MOGO,
The Third Warthog

MOGO,
The Third Warthog

Donna Jo Napoli

illustrated by
Lita Judge

HYPERION BOOKS FOR CHILDREN
NEW YORK
AN IMPRINT OF DISNEY BOOK GROUP

Printed in the United States of America

First Edition

1 3 5 7 9 10 8 6 4 2

Library of Congress Cataloging-in-Publication Data on file.

ISBN 978-1-4231-0816-0

Reinforced binding

Visit www.hyperionbooksforchildren.com

To Elena, who loves warthogs
−DJN

For my dear friend Sy
−LJ

Thanks to my family, especially, and to Anna Cohen, Libby Crissey, Elias and Kristin Lindgren, Meaghan McCans, Suzanna Penikis, and Richard Tchen. Thanks to Celeste Gerhab's fifth grade class at the Swarthmore-Rutledge School in spring, 2006. Thanks to Ben White's seventh and eighth grade English classes at the Webb School in spring, 2006. And a huge thank-you to Namrata Tripathi, my gentle editor.

—DJN

CONTENTS

MOGO,
The Third Warthog

CHAPTER ONE

Last in Line

OF."

I woke with a start. A hoof was jammed into my belly. I wriggled away from my pile of siblings and rolled onto my other side.

Smelly heat made my eyelids flutter. Smelly breath.

Someone was standing over me.

And something was tickling my leg. A tail tassel, for sure.

Others stirred. Churring noises livened the air.

I let out a half-sigh, half-groan. Too bad: morning had come.

It was hard to say good-bye to night—I loved it so. Nighttime meant sleeping warm and cozy with six other warthog bodies over and under and beside me. Everyone safe.

Morning meant daytime. Daytime was anything but safe for piggies.

"Food," someone whispered with need.

"Food, food, food," came the murmured chant of my siblings.

Outside might be danger, but outside was also breakfast. Hunger ruled. I opened my eyes wide to the dark air.

I lifted my rump and rose on my hind legs. Then I crowded with my two sisters and three brothers at the bottom opening of our burrow tunnel. Mother was already outside.

The chanting stopped and silence now sealed us inside our burrow. We waited, so tense and tight I felt others' skin rippling around me.

Sure enough, soft low grunts soon came down the tunnel. Mother was telling us it was safe.

We emerged one by one, blinking in happy relief. The sun streamed down boldly. We trotted after Mother in customary file.

"Out of my way." Gikuyu pushed to the front. He was the only male from last year's litter, so he led, with his littermate sisters behind him: Makena and Wanjiro. One two three, always in that order.

Behind that young litter trotted the older litter—my litter. All three of us were male. Kebiro came first. He was born the biggest. Then Mathani. Then me—Mogo. I was born the runt.

The funny thing was, I had grown as large as my littermates. But our rank order stayed the same, no matter what: Kebiro was brother one, Mathani was brother two, and I was brother three.

Since Mother went first, followed by the younger litter, then followed by my litter, it meant I went very last of all.

I hated being last.

Lions, cheetahs, leopards, wild dogs, spotted hyenas, even Martial eagles went for the last in line.

On the other hand, I wouldn't have wanted one of my siblings to wind up last.

The sad fact was: someone had to be last.

Someone had to be the target.

This baffled me—a true conundrum. I thought about it every morning as we exited our burrow. There was no way out of it.

Mother, Gikuyu, Makena, Wanjiro, Kebiro, Mathani, me. That was the order, every day, everywhere we went.

Now I rushed in line and pressed my flat face against Mathani's rump.

"Watch it, Mogo." He made a gruff noise deep in his throat.

I didn't back off, though. I had just had a new thought. From a distance, with my head up against Mathani like that, it would be hard to distinguish one piggy from another. Maybe a lion would think we two were really one huge animal. No lion would attack such a fierce creature.

"I mean it," said Mathani. He grumbled louder.

I angled my head so that my tusks didn't poke my brother. There was no point making him mad. He could fight hard. And recently my litter brothers had become quick to jump into a brawl.

Being close like this made the heat more

noticeable. The sun already baked us. And there was something different in the air. It shimmered.

"What's wrong with the air?" I said to Mathani.

"Nothing."

"That's not true. It's weird. It gives me the jitters."

Kebiro looked back at me from in front of Mathani. "Everything gives you the jitters, Mogo."

"You're a scaredy," said Mathani.

I lifted my head high. "I'm cautious." Attention to details mattered. Inattentive animals got eaten. I had seen it before.

We met up with my two aunts and their piglets in the dry grasses. All together there were nineteen of us. That was a substantial sounder of warthogs. It was okay to mill around when there were so many of us. Predators got confused by milling piggies. Without a line, it wasn't obvious which one should be the target. I liked feeding with my sounder.

Sniff sniff sniff.

This was a good spot. In a flash we piglets and sows dug with our wide snouts.

"Eat," shouted Kebiro, as though our hungry

sounder needed an order. He stuffed his mouth with roots.

"The deeper ones are tastier," I called.

"Bah!" said Kebiro. "You always think you've got a better way, Mogo. But I'm already eating and you're not."

"Boars bicker," said Mother, coming closer. "That's how warthogs are. Sensible sows never stand in the way of nature's rules, and I am a sensible sow. But the important thing at the moment is to get your bellies full. Eat now. Bicker later."

"Eat then bicker," I said obediently. "Eat then bicker." In fact, though, I didn't care to bicker, now or later. I decided to keep my distance from my brothers for a while.

I wandered in a wide arc at the edge of the sounder, sniffing hard. It would be a pity to eat just any old roots, when there might be something terrific if I searched a moment longer.

"Hey, Mogo." It was my cousin Wambui. Her beady eyes shined at me. I loved that about warthog heads: our eyes were so high and far back in our skulls that we could dig and still look around.

"Aren't you hungry?" she called. "Get down on your front knees and dig."

I gazed across my sounder happily. All those barrel bodies with rumps high in the air. Such a pleasing sight. Warthogs really were the best creatures alive. I looked back at Wambui. "It's not knees, actually, it's wrists."

"Well, I know that. But we talk about kneeling, not wristing. You're such a stickler for details." Wambui chomped on a root. "Get down and eat. There's a ton of roots here."

"I prefer rhizomes."

"Huh?" Wambui stopped rutting. A glob of dirt sat on her snout. She snorted it off. "What're those?"

Wambui was a year younger than me. But, still, her question surprised me. She wasn't the brightest piglet.

"You know how some plants have a big fleshy part right below the ground but above the roots?" I said. "That's a rhizome. If you eat roots, the plants don't grow back. But if you eat rhizomes, the plants come back even more."

Wambui had stopped listening and gone back to chomping. Her attention span had never been impressive. "Hmmm." Her face took on a dreamy glow. "Roots. Ahhh. Roots." She gobbled in a growing stupor.

Grunts of satisfaction came from all around. We warthogs are enthusiastic eaters. My mouth watered. I had better find rhizomes fast.

A flock of creamy-bellied oxpeckers descended on our sounder. They landed lightly on our rumps and pecked greedily. Everyone was greedy when the sun was that hot and the world was that dry. But oxpeckers—they were the greediest. I'd never liked them. Sure, they ate our nasty ticks. But then they stuck their red-and-yellow beaks into the wound and drank warthog blood.

One landed on me. I stamped. It didn't budge. I swatted with my tail tassel. It hopped onto one of my cousins.

This was another conundrum. Now the bird would drink my cousin's blood. And when she drove it off, it would drink another cousin's blood. There was no way to drive the birds off from all of us at once.

I sniffed along the ground till—yes! Turmeric right below the surface—the perfect rhizome breakfast. I sank to my wrists with my trotters pointing backward, and dug and ate. The dry season had been going on for a long time, but still these rhizomes were juicy. And all rhizomes are nutritious. That was how I had grown bigger and stronger than anyone expected of a runt; I ate rhizomes. I watched my oldest aunt eat them, and then did the same. After all, she hadn't become the oldest aunt by accident.

The rhizomes were so abundant here, it was easiest to simply keep my lower tusks in the dirt and plow from one spot to another. So I shuffled along on my front wrists. Shuffling didn't hurt; thick calluses padded my wrists, like on the wrists of all warthogs. What a super feeding place. I wished it was all ours.

Mother must have had the same idea, for she ambled in a big circle, spraying urine here and there. Saliva hung from her lower lip, she was so excited. She ran up to a rock and drooled on it. If any other warthogs were to come along, those smells would tell them this was our sounder's territory.

Watching her, I felt a new sensation. My eyes blurred momentarily. Without thinking, I went over to another rock and rubbed oil from my tusk and eye glands onto it. The rock smelled of me now. A shiver of excitement shot up the back of my neck and shook my mane. I had never helped Mother mark territory before, but this was fun. I pranced from rock to rock on my long legs. And, look at that! I stood taller than Mother, so I left markings even higher. Wow.

An oxpecker hissed. Instantly, several hissed at once.

From out of nowhere a tawny streak came racing. A lioness! Pandemonium struck: warning grunts, a noisy flap of rising oxpecker gray, the dust-thin rumble of hog hooves. We dashed as a unit, tails straight up. Frenzy exaggerated our senses, smothering us with the stench of blood breath at our heels. We ran for dear life.

A second lioness came from the side. And a third.

They surrounded a piglet. One of them clipped the piglet's ankle with a swipe of her claws. The piglet went rolling.

I couldn't see where she landed, I was running so hard.

CHAPTER TWO

Run and Dodge

PIGLETS tumbled headfirst down the closest burrow.

Mother followed on our heels. She did an about-face at the last moment and backed in, squealing at the top of her lungs and threatening the world outside with her lower tusks. I couldn't see her face, of course, but I knew she looked fierce to any creature that dared to peer down the hole. That was because she *was* fierce. A warthog always thought first of escape. But we weren't afraid to fight if we had to, and our lower canines could slice right through a lion paw.

That didn't mean all lionesses backed off, though. Young ones were sometimes too stupid to know better. And old ones were sometimes too desperate to take heed. Mother had warned us of both. In an all-out fight between a mature sow and a lioness, it could be a close call.

Mother stopped shuffling backward and squealed ever louder.

Piglets bashed around in the dark burrow, snorting in panic.

I stood still right behind Mother. With a gulp, I realized that if a lioness dragged her out, I was next in line.

This was not a good thought.

I was not brave. I never wanted to fight anyone for anything.

But I stayed put at Mother's rear. I didn't know what else to do. And when I didn't know what to do, my rule was to wait. This strategy had kept me alive so far.

Pretty soon the energy inside the burrow

died down. No one moved anymore.

After a long while Mother turned around. She huffed and puffed.

My whiskers twitched in worry. "Are you injured?" I whispered.

"Just tired." Mother pushed past. As she moved away from the tunnel opening, light entered the burrow, showing her outline. Big and round.

Oh, dear. Warthogs are not fat as a rule. But Mother was now undeniably fat. Come to think of it, my aunts were, too. No wonder Mother was puffing.

"Time for roll call." Mother's voice trembled.

"We're all here." Kebiro's voice came from the dark behind me. He was the dominant piglet from the older litter; it was right that he should speak up first. "Mathani and Mogo and me. Our litter survived."

"Good," said Mother. "And Gikuyu?" she called.

"We're all here, too," called back Gikuyu. "Makena and Wanjiro and me. Our litter survived, too. We're nestled in a second chamber. A cozy one."

"My girls are safe," Mother said softly.

She must have seen that little female knocked off her hooves by the lioness. I quivered. From the silence in the burrow, I knew the others had seen, too.

Mother stepped toward Gikuyu's voice. I went beside her. I could just make out the three faces of my younger siblings, squashed side by side. They stared down at us in fright.

"You're in a nursery chamber," said Mother in surprise. "You haven't been in a nursery chamber since you were infants." She burst out laughing. "Look at you big overgrown babies, jammed up on that ledge. Come on down."

"A nursery chamber? Oh!" Gikuyu jumped down.

My sisters, Makena and Wanjiro, followed.

"We didn't know." Wanjiro shifted from hoof to hoof.

"It just seemed natural." Gikuyu bobbed his big head.

"Why are nursery chambers high like that?" I asked.

"In case of flooding," said Mother.

"Flooding?" Gikuyu snuffled Mother's neck. "What are you talking about? The world is too dry."

"Right now. But that will change when the rainy season comes again. Which reminds me: I'm thirsty."

"Me, too," came the chorus of my siblings.

I wasn't. And they shouldn't have been, either. Warthogs could go without drinking for weeks at a time. Just that morning we had gotten plenty of liquid from our food. My rhizomes had been downright juicy.

Besides, the idea of going for water now gave me the willies. "It's strange to go to the water hole in the hottest part of the day. Isn't it?"

"Well . . ." Mother's voice drifted vaguely. "At least we'll have it all to ourselves." She went up the tunnel and disappeared outside.

My siblings pressed past me to the mouth of the tunnel and waited impatiently for Mother's signal to emerge.

But my hesitancy grew. Something Mother had said disturbed me. My head spun from the strain of trying to remember.

Oh, yes, she had talked about the rainy season.

Rain. Water from the sky. Running through showers. I remembered it now. Long, long ago.

Rain was nice.

So the rains would start again. Well, that was good.

But Mother also talked about floods. Floods meant lots of water. Lots and lots. Yikes. I didn't want to drown. I didn't want any of us to drown.

"How come we don't have a ledge to sleep on in most of our burrows?" I asked in dismay.

"We're not babies," said Gikuyu. "I'll never go in a nursery chamber again. That was a mistake. Never again," he muttered. "Nope, never."

"But anyone could drown in a flood, not just infants," I said.

"That's you, isn't it, Mogo?" said Kebiro. "Always with the jitters."

"We should dig out high chambers in all our burrows," I said. "We could—"

"Bah!" said Kebiro sharply. "Forget it, Mogo."

Just then Mother's soft, low, beckoning grunts floated down the tunnel.

We filed out, looking around warily. The

distant smell of lion made our sparse hairs stiffen.

"Don't worry," said Mother. "No one will chase us. Feeding lions give all their attention to the meat."

"So they did kill someone." Kebiro's voice was as high and tight as my heart.

"Two piglets." Mother swung her head sadly. "It happens. Every sounder loses piglets toward the end of the dry season."

"Our poor cousins," moaned Wanjiro.

"None of that," said Mother. "No crying. No long faces." She held her own heavy head high. "Warthogs can't afford to waste energy over the inevitable. Just let it be a lesson, so it won't have been for naught."

"A lesson of what?" asked Makena.

"When it's been dry too long, there's extra danger. Predators are so hungry they'll come after anyone—even fighters as strong as warthogs."

"So what are we to do?" asked Kebiro.

"Run and dodge, and run and dodge, and run and dodge." Mother had told us that many times in the past. It was a good rule. I loved it. "Come with me now. Keep your spirits strong. And stay alert."

I remembered my cousin Wambui, blithely gorging on roots, the least alert little warthog I knew. In that dreamy state, how could she run and dodge? A lump formed in my throat.

The rest of our sounder—or what remained of it—joined us. Thirst seemed to have hit everyone at once.

The sun was so high overhead by now, Mother hardly cast a shadow. None of us did. Not a single shadow offered respite from the dazzling heat. That meant we couldn't walk in the shadow of the piggy ahead. Plus our bodies gave off heat of their own.

For a moment I envied hippos and water buffaloes and every other animal that has sweat glands. I bet they didn't suffer from the heat as bad as we did. This was stifling. Still, those animals were clumsy and ugly, so on the whole, it was better to be a warthog. At least we were agile and good-looking.

We piggies naturally spread out a little, just to ease breathing.

And that meant it was even more important to be extra alert.

I swung my head from side to side, just like

Mother, just like my siblings. We were high spirited, and we were alert, even if we were sweltering.

Bitter, yellowed grasses covered the savanna. The only green thing was a stand of acacia trees at a distance. Oh my. I looked around again. Nowhere to hide.

"Run and dodge," I said to Mathani. "Run and dodge," I called to Kebiro. "Run and dodge." No lions would get us.

"Don't tell me what to do," called back Kebiro. "I tell *you*. Run and dodge."

"Run and dodge in this heat?" Mathani stamped a hoof grumpily. "How far do you think we'll get before we tucker out?"

I thought about the water ahead. And now I longed for water, too. I needed to drink and wallow.

A shadow made me look up.

In an instant the giant Martial eagle swooped down on Wanjiro and seized her in his talons. "Got you!" screamed the eagle.

I stood aghast. Wanjiro, my littlest sister!

And it hit me: Wanjiro was the smallest of us piggies, but she was still quite a bundle. I couldn't believe my eyes. How could the bird rise, carrying her weight? We were witnessing a feat that went against nature.

Mother was the first to snap out of the shock. She roared and ran under the flapping wings. But the bird was already too high. My sister's legs pumped futilely in the air.

Wanjiro wriggled and squirmed. She tossed her head, trying her best to slash with those small tusks. Then she went limp.

Oh, no!

But the bird wasn't rising anymore—no, that bird was struggling—he couldn't stay aloft much longer.

"Kick, Wanjiro!" I shouted. "Kick!"

The Martial eagle glared down at me. "Shut up!" he screamed.

Wanjiro gave a final twist and kick . . . and she dropped. Free! She hit the ground and rolled and got up running and squealing at the top of her lungs.

The eagle flew off.

Mother let out an explosive grunt and she and Wanjiro ran straight for each other. They touched snout-to-snout in relief and joy.

"I knew it," I said happily.

"Knew what?" asked Mathani.

"That bird couldn't get enough lift with Wanjiro in his talons."

"You think you're so smart." Kebiro lowered his forehead. "I ought to ram you."

But before he could do it, a hyena came racing through the brush straight for Makena, my other sister, and the next smallest among us. That was what all that commotion had done—attracted a filthy hyena. We had probably woken him from a midday nap. And the rest of the pack couldn't be far behind.

Such bad luck was too much. We all squealed now, all raced for the closest burrow, tails straight up. Run and dodge. Hyena jaws! They crunch through bones and hooves and even teeth. Run and dodge.

But Mother turned and charged the hyena. Had she gone mad? She couldn't possibly win against a hyena pack.

And what now? The hyena turned and slunk into the brush he came from. The spots on the hyena's sloped back blended with the grasses till he was lost to sight.

Then nothing.

It was over. All the terrible, terrifying chaos—over. Just like that.

Saved from the strongest talons. Saved from the strongest jaws. Over and done.

I didn't know how Mother had recognized this hyena as a loner, but once again I was reminded: Mother was brilliant. Mother kept us safe.

Still, we galloped the rest of the way to the water hole.

Mother's words resounded in my head: when it's been dry too long, there's extra danger.

Boy, was that the truth.

CHAPTER THREE

The Water Hole

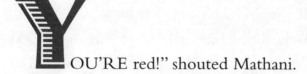

OU'RE red!" shouted Mathani.

"I am not; you are!" shouted back Kebiro.

They rolled in the muddy water hole, bashing each other. When they finally stopped for a breath, I grunted. "You're both red."

"That eagle was right when he told you to shut up, Mogo." Kebiro glared at me. "So shut up. Or I'll smash you. Besides, you're red."

"We're all red," I said. "Look down at yourself."

Kebiro and Mathani looked at their front legs.

"I don't want to be red," Mathani whined.

Kebiro blew mud off his lips and turned to me. "I didn't know I was red. Mathani didn't know he was red. So how did you know you were red, Mogo?"

I lay down, rolled slowly all the way over, and stood up again. "See? The mud's red. So we're red."

"You think you're so smart, don't you, Mogo?" Kebiro lowered his head for battle.

"No I don't," I said quickly. "I'm just a piggy, like you. A mud-loving, red piggy."

Wanjiro swung her head toward us. "Red as the belly of a malachite kingfisher bird."

"And almost as bright as his bill," added Makena. She gave us an approving glance. "Don't you think they're handsome, Wanjiro? I bet female piggies are going to like our big brothers someday soon."

We brothers straightened up at Makena's words. We tried to strut, but the mud slowed us down.

We went back to wallowing, the whole sounder, squealing and snorting and grunting. We filled the water hole. There was no room for other creatures. But it didn't matter, because no one else came. Everyone with any sense was off in the shade, escaping the sun.

Even predators were sleeping.

But they could be woken. Like that rotten hyena.

I jumped to attention.

"Shhh, quiet, everyone."

"Why?" asked Mathani.

"Predators."

"There you go again," said Kebiro. "You dwell on danger. There's something wrong with your brain, Mogo. No doubt about it."

"Yeah," said Mathani. "Don't be dumb, Mogo. There's no one around to bother us."

"How can you say that? Lions, eagles, hyenas. What more do you need in a single day?"

"Exactly," said Kebiro. "We've already had more than our share of bad luck. Nothing else bad can happen today."

"I don't think that's how it works," I said. "It's not like the predators get together and agree to lay off 'cause we've already been attacked three times."

Without warning, Kebiro charged me. His huge wide face smacked against mine. Our upper tusks clacked.

Kebiro backed off.

I was still standing, dizzy, but unhurt.

It was moments like this when I understood the value of facial warts. Ours had grown into big, pointy cones. Prominent warts cushioned blows and protected our eyes and jaw. Even when adult males fought during mating season they rarely hurt each other.

I was about to turn away when Kebiro came racing for a second blow. *Clack!*

I cried out, "Stop already."

"Someone needs to shut you up. I say nothing else bad can happen today. So that's that."

The sound of a zebra herd made us look around in surprise. Most zebras had left the area months before, when the water holes grew scarce. Mother told us they had migrated to the valley where the lakes were, so they could drink deep and daily.

This pathetic-looking little herd had gotten left behind. Poor things. The stallion's ribs stuck out.

The two mares, two fillies, and a colt staggered, they were so weak. They looked defenseless without a big herd around them. I hoped the other zebras would come back when the rains returned. Not just for this tiny herd's sake, but because I liked zebras. I liked their musty smell. I liked their funny noises.

"Hello," I called.

"My harem." The stallion pawed at the mud. His voice was dry and thin and hardly more than a whisper. "My harem. Mine." He threw his head back and looked me in the eye. "Mine mine mine." He talked so fast, his lips made a popping noise.

The foolish thing, as though any of us warthogs would have wanted to butt in on zebra mares. This heat had made him batty. I moved away from him.

They drank, front hooves in the mud, lined up perfectly beside one another. I liked that about zebras, too; they were organized.

Once they had had their fill, the little ones perked up. It was as though the muddy water had performed a miracle. They cantered in circles, nipping and kicking at the air, making sweet, high-pitched noises.

"Grass," crooned a filly. "Think of eating heavenly grass again."

"Bulbs," whistled the other filly.

"Rhizomes," grunted the colt.

"Shoots," called the first filly, louder now.

"Buds," sang the other filly even louder.

"Fruits," shouted the colt. "Fruits, fruits, fruits."

That final thought seemed to send them into ecstasy. They banged into each other and galloped wildly.

The two mares ignored the whole thing. They stood side by side, one facing the opposite direction of the other, and, with teeth and thick, blubbery lips, each nibbled and scraped along the

other's neck and shoulder and back. Grooming.

A pang of longing reverberated in my chest. I wanted to be groomed that way, too. Warthogs groomed each other, sure. If I lay on my tummy or sprawled on one side, pretty soon someone would come along and strip my mane through his incisors. But what these zebras were doing looked far better. They didn't have upper and lower tusks to get in the way of their muzzles. I watched closely.

The young ones stopped playing for a moment. They stood, muzzles together, sides heaving from the exertion.

I stepped toward a filly with a friendly swagger, and offered my mane for grooming.

"Hold it right there, buddy." The colt rolled his lips away from his teeth and spread his jaw. "Yeah yeah, I see those tusks. But have you ever been bit by a zebra?" He turned his haunches to me and looked back over his shoulder. "I kick, too. You stay away from Dad's mares and you stay away from my sisters."

"Get back here, Mogo," called Mother.

But I had already backtracked. I could do without a zebra grooming. Zebras might play nice together, but not with anyone else. Plus the males seemed positively demented.

Mathani made a disgusted grunt. "What's the matter with you, Mogo?"

"Warthogs are warthogs and zebras are zebras," said Kebiro. "You may talk smart, Mogo, but you act dumb." He head-butted me again.

"Ah, you're practicing." Mother slogged through the mud. "That's good."

"Practicing? What would we be practicing for?" asked Mathani.

"Standing up for yourselves."

"The sounder stands up for us," said Kebiro.

"Not for long," said Mother. "You're going to be on your own soon."

"We are?" I squeaked in shock.

Mother threw me a disapproving glance. "When the rains come, I'll go off and find a nice aardvark burrow, like usual, and widen it out. I'll make a high nursery chamber, too. And I'll have my next litter."

"Your next litter?" Makena came up beside Mother. "Baby piggies?"

It all made sense now—that was why Mother

had grown fat. That was why she was tired and thirsty all the time.

Delight filled me. It would be fun to have new piglets around again.

"When they're several weeks old," said Mother, "I'll bring them back with me and join you three again."

"Three?" Delight disappeared. Horror gripped my heart. "There are six of us," I squeaked.

Mother threw me another disapproving glance.

By this time Wanjiro and Gikuyu had come to join the conversation.

Mother turned to them. "Gikuyu and Makena and Wanjiro, you'll meet the new litter. We'll be happy together."

"What about me?" asked Kebiro.

"You and Mathani and Mogo are big now. Too big to stay in the sounder."

"Too big to stay in the sounder?" I squeaked.

"Really, Mogo," said Mother, finally turning to me. "You're too old for such squeaks. You three are grown up."

"But what will we do?" asked Kebiro.

"Build your own homes," said Mother.

34

"Just the three of us?" I squeaked. Already I missed my sounder.

"No," said Mother. "Each one of you will make a home. You'll live alone. Sows are social. We form sounders. But boars aren't. Boars live solitary lives."

"I'm social," I squeaked.

Mother frowned at me.

"I'm social," I said again, in as normal a voice as I could muster.

"That's because you're still thinking like a piglet. But you boys are boars now. Look at the way you charge each other all the time. You have to leave."

"I'll dig out a nursery chamber for you in the new burrow," I said. "I was going to offer that anyway. And . . ."

"I can dig my own nursery chamber."

"But . . ."

"There are no buts about it."

"But . . ."

"Hush! That's that!" Mother flopped in the mud.

Kebiro and Mathani and I stared at her. Then we stared at each other.

Kebiro was wrong; something else bad had happened today. Something really bad. Normally, I would have rubbed that in. But right then I didn't have the heart.

CHAPTER FOUR

Out in the Rain

THE OTHERS slept like normal, in a big pile. But nothing was normal anymore. Everything was terrible. Or about to become terrible.

I lay down and fretted. But the comfort of my siblings' bodies soon drew me in. Yes, that comfort would be gone when the rains came. Now, though, it soothed me in spite of myself.

Rain, rain, stay away, I sang inside my head. Never come back. Never never.

★ ★ ★

I woke to an insistent and unfamiliar excitement. Instantly I knew something had happened overnight. Something big. My siblings knew, too. We huddled close. Anticipation hung in the air.

But it wasn't just anticipation. Something else was in the air. No doubt about it; the air had changed. The day before it had been weird. But this morning it was even weirder. There was a weight to it. I opened my mouth. The air sat on my tongue like a living thing. Like a stunned grub. I could almost eat it.

It was darker than usual. No morning sun filtered in through the tunnel mouth. What was wrong with the sun?

The burrow smelled different, too. The dirt itself gave off an odor. Every warthog had a keen sense of smell, but this sensation wasn't because my snout was so good. The dirt was pungent.

I backed up a little. A clump of dirt stuck to one hoof. I couldn't remember the last time burrow dirt stuck in my hooves. The ground below us wasn't rock-hard anymore.

Then I heard it. Little thuds from above.

This burrow wasn't our favorite. We had gone to our favorite the evening before, only to find that another family from our sounder had already occupied it. First come, first served—that was the rule. So we settled for this burrow—which was more shallow than most. The surface was so close above us that we could hear those thuds from outside, as though grasshoppers danced up there. Zillions of them.

Hey, maybe those big blue-and-yellow ones had come back. They were cool. I used to hop after them when I was Gikuyu's age.

Grasshoppers were good. And delicious.

Thud thud thud thud thud.

We waited, our ears straining past those little thuds to try to make out Mother's grunts that would tell us it was safe to come out.

We waited and fidgeted and shoved in and around each other.

Stomachs growled.

Where was Mother?

The pressure on my bladder grew. I had to stay very still or I would have an accident.

Everyone was suddenly very still.

"Let's go out," came a voice in the dark at last. It was Kebiro.

"You first," came Gikuyu's voice.

That made sense. Kebiro was the dominant one of the older litter. If anyone had to go out first, it should be him.

Nobody else volunteered. That made sense, too. After all, exiting from a burrow is the most dangerous part of a warthog's day. Who knew what creature might lie in ambush out there?

Slow steps went up the tunnel and faded.

Kebiro was brave.

A few seconds later Kebiro shouted from above, "Come out, come out!"

"What do we do?" quivered Mathani's voice through the dark.

"He doesn't sound scared," came Wanjiro's voice. "Do you think he sounds scared? He doesn't, right?"

"Don't ask me," said Mathani. "I'm not the dominant boar. Kebiro is."

"What do we do? Oh, what do we do?" came Makena's voice. She let out a distress churr. "What do you think, Mogo?"

My breath caught. No one had ever asked my advice before.

"Why ask Mogo?" came Mathani's voice, with an edge of jealousy.

"You just said you didn't want to be asked," said Makena. "Make up your mind."

"Ask me, ask me, ask me," whined Mathani. "I want to be asked, after all."

"Sorry, but we need to hear Mogo's opinion, anyway," piped up little Wanjiro. "You can grumble all you want, Mathani, but Mogo is the most cautious. We all know that. And he figures things out. So . . . what do you think, Mogo?"

I didn't know what I thought. Which, of course, meant we should wait. On the other hand, our bladders were full and our tummies weren't.

"Come on, you dummies. What are you waiting for?" called Kebiro, as if in answer to my very thoughts. "Get out here. This is terrific."

"Let's go," I said decisively.

We scooted up the tunnel.

And out into . . . water! Water fell from the sky everywhere. We lifted our snouts and water ran up our nostrils till we sneezed. Rain! This was what I remembered. Rain. It came down in little thuds. That was the noise we had heard from the burrow. Rain. It cooled my back. I lowered myself to the ground and rolled over. It cooled my belly.

I got to my hooves and frolicked with my siblings. We trotted. We cantered. We galloped.

We came across a series of depressions in the ground that were already filling with rainwater. We stamped through the puddles. We splashed each other.

I didn't know how long we had been fooling around like that when it hit me: Mother was nowhere around. The rest of our sounder was nowhere around. We were alone. Piggies out in the rain. No loving eyes keeping watch. Anything could get us.

"We have to find Mother," I screeched.

But my siblings ignored me. Even Makena, who just a little earlier had sought my advice. Even Wanjiro, who had praised my caution.

"We need Mother. We need protection. We need love." I raced around them. "Mother, Mother, Mother!"

"Stop running, Mogo," Kebiro said sternly.

I stopped and waited.

Kebiro walked off.

Everyone else fell into line behind him, as though he was in charge now. Kebiro, then the younger litter, then Mathani. They acted as though they had already accepted the idea that Mother was gone.

This was worse than if they had cried.

Where was Mother?

She couldn't really have run off.

Could she?

She said she'd leave. But she would have given us more warning. She would have said goodbye. She wouldn't just have disappeared. Not the mother I knew. Not that brilliant sow.

Oh no! A predator must have gotten her.

I sniffed, and almost choked on rain. It was impossible to smell lions in this downpour.

So that meant it was impossible for lions to smell warthogs, too.

So Mother was fine. She had to be. And she would come back for us. She knew where we were. All we needed to do was wait. "Wait," I shouted to my siblings.

But they were moving away fast. This was a terrible conundrum. If I left with my siblings, Mother might never find us again. But if I stayed behind, I'd be all alone.

Alone was so bad I couldn't bear to imagine it. I raced to catch up.

"Wait," I said, as I reached them. "We should just . . ."

"I say what we should do, Mogo," said Kebiro. "Me. Not you." He lowered his head as if to charge.

I swallowed my words and fell into last place in line.

Kebiro followed the string of puddles and we followed Kebiro. I looked over my shoulder regularly, but Mother never appeared.

Soon we saw a black rhino standing at the end of the puddle string.

Kebiro stopped short. We all did.

The rhino held his head high, and the little point on his upper lip wiggled in the air like a baboon finger. He was clearly enjoying the rain. It was his footprints that had made the puddles we'd been following. Even though black rhinos are smaller than white ones, they're still huge, with feet as wide as my legs were long.

I wasn't crazy about rhinos. They lived alone, except for the occasional herd of females with their young. And when black rhinos sensed danger, they charged. But something inside me was glad to see this one. The strangest idea came to me.

"Let's stick by him," I blurted out.

Kebiro glowered at me fiercely.

"He's a rhino, you dummy," said Mathani. "See the horns on his nose?"

"He's fierce," said Gikuyu. "Even lions wouldn't come near a healthy rhino."

"Right," I said. "Precisely." I looked at Kebiro, waiting a moment for the words to sink in. "What should we do, Kebiro?" I asked demurely. "How can we stay safe?"

Kebiro's eyes narrowed. He tilted his head in thought. "Hmm. I have an idea. The rhino's here; we're here. I always say, 'When opportunity knocks . . .'"

"I never heard you say that," said Wanjiro.

"Well, I'm saying it now. Let's stay with this rhino."

"Isn't that what Mogo suggested?" said Wanjiro.

Kebiro ignored her.

We moved carefully toward the rhino.

He swiveled one ear, but otherwise gave us no heed. He walked along leisurely, munching yellowed bush leaves.

We watched those chewing jaws enviously. Finally, we gave in to our hunger and dug up bulbs and roots, checking the rhino warily at regular intervals. When he did nothing new, we grunted and abandoned ourselves to gobbling.

Everyone except me, that is. I ate, sure, but I also studied the rhino. Up close like this, I saw things that didn't show from a distance. And I liked what I saw. His skin was the same gray as ours, now that the rain had washed the red mud off us. And he was sparsely haired, with only a fringe of ear whiskers. We warthogs had scattered whiskers across our cheeks, a line of brown hair that formed our manes, and our little white beards. But that was all. Yes, this rhino was pleasingly hairless. He had a tail tassel and so did we. His teeth were grinders like most of ours. And those two nose horns were practically as nice as warts.

"You're a good-looking guy," I said to the

rhino. "For someone who isn't a warthog, that is. Just a bit on the gigantic side."

"What are you doing?" Kebiro butted me in the side. "Do you have to try to talk to everyone? What did I tell you when you talked to the zebras? Huh? What did I tell you? I'm in charge here. Warthogs and rhinos don't talk to each other. So you shut up."

I looked at the rhino to see what he thought of all this.

The rhino stood still with his head raised, alert. He didn't seem to be listening to us at all, but to something else entirely, something out there, beyond us.

"What's the matter?" whispered Wanjiro. "Do you think he senses danger?"

I looked around. The rain drummed steadily. I couldn't see far. There was no telling where a predator might be.

A crazy urge came to me. I ran under the rhino, giddy with my own rashness. Right between his front legs.

"What are you doing?" gasped Mathani.

"I'm a baby rhino."

"You're a nutcase," said Kebiro.

"Don't you think I look like a baby rhino? From a distance? Through the rain? What predator would dare attack baby rhinos under their daddy's belly?"

My siblings gawked. But one by one they crowded under the rhino's belly.

We waited, peering through the rain as best we could. But nothing happened. No scary predator passed.

The rhino made a raspy noise. Again and again. Regular as a heartbeat. Oh! I knew what was regular as a heartbeat. I stepped out from underneath him and looked up at his face to be sure. "He's snoring," I said. "He fell asleep standing up!"

"That's crazy," said Makena. "Rhinos lie down to nap."

"What do we do now?" asked Gikuyu.

"If he feels safe enough to sleep, that's good," said Kebiro. He walked out into the rain and dug for food.

So did everyone else.

Me last.

After a while, the rain stopped, and the sun and gentle wind dried us. We grazed beside the rhino a long time, lulled by the sweet weather.

It was late afternoon when I spied something in a nearby fig tree. For a second, I didn't realize what I was seeing. But then it hit hard: a cheetah. Her tail hung down in plain view.

My own tail shot straight up. I ran to the other side of the rhino. My siblings' tails shot straight up. They ran to the other side of the rhino.

We clustered in stupefied silence. How dumb

could we have been not to smell that cheetah? It was because of the rain, I was sure, even though it wasn't coming down anymore; it had washed her scent from the grasses. And the wind blew toward her, robbing our noses.

That cheetah definitely was close enough to tell warthogs from baby rhinos.

We were targets.

With no idea where the closest burrow was.

The only thing between us and that cheetah was this rhino. This sleeping rhino.

I peeked around the rhino at the cheetah. She was looking in our direction, with those high-set eyes. Black lines ran from the corners of her eyes down the sides of her nose to her mouth. Her head was small and mean. When she saw me peeking, she hissed. My stomach flipped.

The rhino's round ears swiveled toward that hiss. So he was awake now. He bit off another swatch of leaves and chewed slowly. Was he blind? He acted as though he didn't see the cheetah.

If that cat came at us, what could we do? Run and dodge. No. Outrunning a lioness is one thing. But the cheetah is the fastest hunter in Africa.

Mother would have known what to do. Mother knew what to do when the hyena attacked. Mother always knew what to do.

We were doomed without Mother. "Six doomed piggies," I muttered.

"But good-looking, all the same," said the rhino. "Just a bit on the puny side."

So he did listen to me before. "Can you save us?"

"Not my job," said the rhino. "But I give advice."

"What?" I asked.

"Look big."

I opened my mouth to ask what that meant, when the cheetah leaped from the tree and my throat closed in fear.

My siblings gasped.

The cheetah walked slowly on those long legs.

We piglets crowded under the rhino again.

The sun glistened off the cheetah's claws. In that moment it struck me that that was the creepiest thing about cheetahs; their claws never retracted all the way. It made them look like they were always ready to rip someone apart.

The cheetah walked slower.

We pressed together tighter.

The rhino stopped chewing and swung his big head toward her.

She walked slower still.

Then in a burst, she ran. She ran so fast, all four feet were off the ground at once. She flew.

At the last moment our massive rhino wheeled lightly on his feet and started off in the other direction.

We piggies screamed and scattered, racing to

get out of the way of rhino hooves and cheetah claws.

The cheetah ran past us at the female kudu I saw now for the first time. The doe bounded off. Her newborn fawn was left behind.

"Meat," yowled the cheetah as she pounced.

I ran, tail straight up, screaming. All of us ran, all of our tails straight up, all of us screaming. We ran and ran and plunged down the first burrow entrance we came to.

CHAPTER FIVE

Six Nervous Piggies

LIFE HAD become awful. Mother had been gone for almost three weeks. We piglets were suffering under the strain

All day long Kebiro stamped his hooves as though flies were bothering him. *Stamp stamp.* But there were no flies in this rain. *Stamp stamp stamp.*

Mathani walked in a circle in the mud. Round and round.

Gikuyu slapped the wet tassel of his tail from

one side of his rump to the other. *Slap slap. Slap slap.*

Makena ran her rough lips up and down her forelegs in a futile attempt to groom herself in this sloppy world. Up and down, up and down.

Wanjiro repeatedly opened and closed her jaw with a click, whether she was eating or not. *Click click.*

And I shook. Constantly. *Brrrrrr.*

Six nervous piggies, alone in the world.

Once I spied a lone sow out foraging. Mother? But when I called, she raced away.

A couple of times we were lucky enough to join up with other members of our sounder. But, really, there was nothing lucky about it—it just felt like it should be lucky. Our aunts had disappeared, too. So joining up meant an even larger group of unprotected piggies out in the open.

These were confusing times.

The rainy season turned out to be our enemy. It had taken the mothers away. They were off somewhere with their new babies. We were left on our own.

At the same time, the rainy season was a friend.

There was always new food. After the first heavy rains, mushrooms sprang up in spreading mounds. Delicious insects crawled through grasses, which sprouted green and savory. With the first turn of the dirt, grubs rolled onto our tongues. Previously dry creek beds ran in rivulets, and tall scrumptious sedges lined them. We gobbled. The world grew wetter and cooler and we grew bigger and stronger.

And, despite our newly acquired nervous habits, we grew smarter. Right now we were surrounded by a herd of impalas. That was smart. Our sounder had always grazed in the middle of antelopes, especially impalas, but I had never before thought about why. Piglets just did what the others did, in a reassuring mindlessness.

Now I knew: antelopes stood taller than warthogs, so they saw farther and could give off an alarm signal in plenty of time for us to escape a predator. By now we lone piggies had tried out various species of antelope. The eland stood the tallest, with their big, thick shoulders. We joined them first. I was drawn to them anyway because of their funny twisted horns that rippled dark and light. But the trouble with them was exactly their size; because they were so big, they were prey for the strongest predators—the lions. And warthogs looked puny beside elands, so lions picked us out as the easy targets. We discovered that the first time a lioness chased the herd. If a young eland hadn't been so dazed with fright that she tumbled over a log, Wanjiro would have become lion meat.

Impalas, on the other hand, were perfect. They were taller than warthogs, but so slender and slight that they appeared more vulnerable. Look big. That was what the rhino had said. He was wise. Plenty of predators hunted the impala herds we joined, but we piglets weren't their targets, because, short as we were, our bulk looked big and tough in the midst of a herd of graceful impalas.

And antelopes had the habit of giving birth in the early part of the rainy season. The mother would go off alone, give birth, then return with a tiny fawn—an easy target.

It was horrible to be safe at the expense of the weak. Particularly babies. This might have been the worst conundrum of all. But that was the way it worked on the savanna.

I remembered the pathetic kudu fawn, on

wobbly legs, slick from birth, like a glistening delicacy for that cheetah.

The rules of life and death could be harsh.

But at least Mother's newest piglets weren't out in the open like the kudu fawn. I imagined them tucked up high and dry in a burrow nursery chamber.

Still, I couldn't get the cheetah out of my mind. Those long black lines on her face, like tear streaks, haunted me. I was reminded of her every time I looked at Kebiro and Mathani. They had developed dark stains from their tear glands, running from a big patch under their eyes down the sides of their snouts. Four of their six facial warts were stained. They looked like mature boars now.

I did, too, of course. We were grown up. Mother was right.

But she was only right about our outsides. Inside I was still a bitty piggy. I wanted Mother back. Worry kept me shaking all the time.

And the impalas didn't help when it came to that. They were naturally worried creatures. They hardly ever talked, but when they did it was frantic exchanges like:

"Did you see something?"

"No. Did you?"

"Did you smell something?"

"No. Did you?"

"Did you hear something?"

"No. But let's run anyway, just to be safe."

It was discouraging.

All the same, we stayed with them. It was better than being alone.

The rain stopped. Immediately the temperature rose. Muggy heat cloaked us.

We spread out as we foraged, when, oh! an ostrich came running across the grasses toward the impala herd. Another ran behind it. And several more behind that one. A couple of cocks and a flurry of hens.

Ostriches were tall; the only animals taller than them were elephants and giraffes. So ostriches could spot danger way far away. Fleeing ostriches were an early warning system for everyone.

The impala beside me turned and leaped, sailing high above my head. She landed on all four hooves at once and bounced high again in that strange stotting gait that only impalas do. The whole herd stotted and leaped away now, practically airborne.

We pigs shot our tails up straight and raced squealing after the herd.

But I glanced over my shoulder and stopped short. "Hey," I called to my siblings. "Hey, look. Look at them."

The ostriches had stopped running. Now they twirled in place. Their feathers fluffed out. Their heads swayed precariously on those long necks.

"What are they doing?" said Gikuyu.

"They've gone wacko," said Kebiro.

"I don't like it," said Mathani.

"Maybe they're dancing," said Wanjiro.

We walked cautiously toward the strange birds. Ostriches weren't usually dangerous to warthogs. But those big beaks were powerful. We couldn't risk getting pecked.

The ostriches just kept twirling, though. They seemed delirious. It was a wonderful sight, mesmerizing.

Eventually the birds slowed to a stagger then went back to running across the grasses.

Our eyes followed till they had disappeared. Incredible, like a dream.

The impala herd was long gone by now.

We were suddenly alone. Six piggies out on the savanna.

I looked around anxiously. "Let's go find a burrow."

"Who made you boss?" Kebiro shifted his weight from hoof to hoof, as though he might charge me.

"It won't be evening for a while yet," said Gikuyu, "and I'm still hungry."

"Me, too," said Makena and Wanjiro and Mathani together.

I didn't dare make another suggestion. Not with Kebiro looking at me so mad. And I couldn't think of any clever way to make him decide we should find a burrow. But I had to do something. We couldn't stay alone on this plain. "The impalas are gone," I said meekly.

"That's not the only herd." Kebiro looked across the plain. "We'll find another."

We wandered in the direction the ostriches came from. And there, in front of us, was a second incredible sight. Two lion cubs batted a round, white stone back and forth.

We spun in circles, trying to sight their mother.

One of the cubs noticed us. His gray-blue eyes blinked. They were so different from the evil amber of adult lion eyes, I couldn't help but blink back.

The innocent one ambled toward us with curiosity on his face, half-falling over his big milk belly. "Hi," he called. "Hi, hi."

The other hesitated. Then she sat primly and stared shyly, if that's possible, till she toppled over on her side. "Oops." She scrambled back to her haunches.

They couldn't have been more than a month old.

And the mother wasn't around, or she'd have attacked by now. She must have been a very bad mother. And where was the third cub? There were at least three when it came to lions. Everyone knew that.

The bolder cub suddenly ran back to the stone and batted it straight at Wanjiro. "Catch!" he shouted.

Wanjiro turned tail. The rock hit her in the thigh. "Ouch!"

It broke!

It wasn't a rock at all. It was a giant egg.

"An ostrich egg!" Kebiro whooped. "Like I always say, 'When opportunity knocks . . .'"

All six piglets lapped at the gooey mess, while the male cub ran around us yipping, "Me, too, me, too." But he didn't dare nose in among us.

"Where there's one, there's bound to be more," said Mathani.

"More," said the male cub. He ran and tripped

and landed in a nest. Well, not really a nest. Or, if it was a nest, it was a poor excuse for one. It was only a scrape in the dirt, filled with eggs. Lots of them. I couldn't count that high.

We ate while the cubs wrestled.

The strangeness of the ostrich dance followed by this cozy scene with the lion cubs got to me. Something was wrong about it. Everything was wrong about it. My head spun. Nothing was as expected. The only thing I knew for sure was that the lioness had to be close by. We should leave. Fast.

At that very moment, Mother appeared out of the blue. Our beautiful, brilliant mother.

And she charged us.

CHAPTER SIX

Old Enough

"GO. It's time. Go away." Mother was lodged in the entrance to a burrow, face outward. She had been like this for a long time. Too long.

Mother had separated my litter from the rest when she charged us. She took Gikuyu and Makena and Wanjiro—the younger piggies—down inside that burrow with the new piglets. They were safe.

Kebiro and Mathani and I—the older piggies—

were left outside, standing in front of Mother's face, disbelieving. And anything but safe. It was incomprehensible.

"You can't imagine what we've been through," said Kebiro.

"Without you life is awful," said Mathani.

"We need you," I squeaked. Then I cleared my throat. "We need you," I said in a low voice.

"You might be the stubbornest young boars in the history of Africa," said Mother. "But I won't change my mind. I can't. The system makes sense. It's been working since the beginning of time. There are new piglets now. You are old."

"I'm not old," I chirped.

"You're old enough. Go make your own homes."

"How?" asked Kebiro.

"The way any warthog does. Find an abandoned aardvark burrow. Dig it out wide enough to be comfortable."

"Where?" asked Mathani.

"Anywhere."

My heart fluttered with hope. "You mean we can stay close?"

"You can stay wherever you like. Our sounder shares the home range with two other sounders. And with many single males. That's where the fathers come from, after all. We're a big clan."

A clan. I never knew we formed a clan. I'd seen other sounders from a distance on occasion. But we didn't socialize with them. And of course I'd seen lone males running around.

So they were the fathers.

My own father must have been one of them. Kebiro and Mathani's father, too. Our father.

And somewhere out there was the father of Gikuyu and Makena and Wanjiro.

And, oh, many months before—a good half-year, I'd guess—a male had surprised Mother as she exited the burrow one morning. He must be the father of the newest piglets.

The newest piglets. Ah.

There were four of them. Exactly as many as the number of teats Mother had. And they were darling. I got a good view before those dear piglets rushed down the burrow tunnel with their teeny tails pointing straight up. They were completely hairless. And fat-bellied, like the two lion cubs that played with the ostrich egg. Two males and two females. Plumpty-dumpty darlings. I wanted to roll them over and over in the grasses with my snout. They would be a joy to play with.

"What are their names?" I asked.

Mother sighed. "Don't go thinking about the piglets. I told you. I told you and I told you and I told you. You will never know them. Only two litters stay with the sounder at once. You are now the third litter. You are grown. How many times do I have to say this? Sows can stay forever. But boars can't. All of you are boars, so all of you must leave." She shook her head wearily. "I'm sorry, but this practice makes sense. It's for the good of the sounder."

"Just their names," I begged. "Please."

"There's no point getting attached to them. You must leave."

"Couldn't we stay a little longer?" I asked. "A year, maybe?"

"A year! Mogo, you and your brothers probably won't mate for another couple of years. But you are mature. And bulky. There's not enough room in any burrow for all of us."

"We could dig this burrow out bigger," I said.

"Oh, Mogo." Mother's voice wavered.

"Good," said Kebiro. "Move aside, Mother."

"Yes, yes," said Mathani. "Let us in."

"Go away!" shouted Mother in renewed resolve. "Go away or I'll charge again."

High-pitched cries came from inside the burrow. Mother made the sweetest grunts back. That was how Gikuyu and Makena and Wanjiro used to cry, back when they still nursed. And that was how Mother used to talk with them. I loved that way of talking.

"I have to go feed my babies now," said Mother. "Scat."

"But . . ." I said.

Mother growled. Loud and nasty. A growl, from our own mother.

We jumped backward, and watched with dismay as the tips of her upper tusks disappeared down the tunnel.

"We're on our own," said Kebiro.

"Forever," said Mathani. "Good-bye."

My insides heated up unexpectedly. I wanted to kick something. Or someone. "No," I said.

"No?" asked Kebiro. "No to what?"

"No to everything. No no no."

"Well, that's just stupid," said Mathani. "You can't say no to everything."

"No to splitting up. Let's form a little bachelor group."

"What's gotten into you?" said Mathani. "Didn't you listen? We're each supposed to go off on our own."

"We stuck together when Mother left us before." I became more and more confident as I heard my own words. "We can stick together now. We can stick together forever."

"Only sows and babies stick together forever," said Kebiro. "You're not a sow, so if you want to stick together forever, that means you're a baby. Baby Mogo. Scared all the time."

"Aren't you scared?" I asked.

"I am a boar," Kebiro pronounced solemnly.

"Well, then, what about company? Don't you like company?"

"Boars don't need company," said Mathani, but sadly.

"They might like company, though. I'm sure

there must be other brothers out there who stick together."

"No you're not," said Kebiro. "You've never seen them."

"Well, even so, we can do it." I ran around my brothers. "Who's to stop us?"

No one said anything.

The terrible fact smacked us in the face: there might be no one in the world besides us who cared what we did now.

"We were lucky to be born in a litter of three males," I whispered. "It's like you always say, Kebiro, 'When opportunity knocks . . .'"

Kebiro took a few steps backward. I tightened up, ready to fend off his attack. But then he stepped forward again. "Opportunity," he said a bit doubtfully.

"Right," I murmured. "That's what you always say." I looked over at Mathani. "That's what he always says, right, Mathani?"

Mathani looked at me with troubled eyes. "You have crazy ideas, Mogo."

"It's almost night," I said softly.

Mathani rocked from side to side on his

hooves. "I've never been out at night."

"I bet no warthog has," I said. "It's unheard of."

Mathani moved over beside me and the two of us stood together as a unit before Kebiro.

Kebiro snorted. Then he turned halfway, so that Mathani and I were facing his side. With a gulp I saw how massive Kebiro had become. And in that moment I understood: with that sideways stance, he was displaying his dominance over us in a new way.

Well, that was fine with me. I didn't want to be in charge. All I wanted was for us to stay together. The corners of my mouth quivered from the tension.

"Let's go find a burrow," Kebiro said in a somber voice.

"Yay," I breathed.

"For one night," said Kebiro. "One."

We trotted in line. In this moment I loved following. It was natural. It was normal. I couldn't imagine trotting all alone. For the past three weeks, the whole period that Mother had been gone, Kebiro had led us. He did it well. I never wanted to leave him. Or Mathani. I loved my brothers. I would do anything Kebiro said.

We found a burrow. It was occupied. And the tenant warthogs said, "No extra room." Not for boars, at least.

We found another burrow. More tenant warthogs. More resistance to boars.

We went from burrow to burrow. All were occupied at this time of day. No sow would let us in. No sow had pity on boars.

Dark fell. Warthogs were active only in daytime. I could feel myself slowing down from the inside out. My skin crawled with a sense of impending danger.

Something rustled in the brushes to our right. It was an elephant. Alone. A rogue male? Rogue males sometimes went on the rampage.

We cantered now. We went to every burrow we knew. Faster and faster. We had wasted precious time arguing with Mother. It was so dark now, I couldn't see past Mathani's rump.

Crickets chirped, frogs croaked, zebras whinnied, wildebeests snorted.

Hoots and laughs came from the distance. Dreaded hyenas.

We galloped.

Finally we found an unoccupied burrow. Mathani and I dove in. Kebiro shuffled in backward after us.

We nestled together inside. Safe at last. Gradually my heart beat softer, slower.

It was odd not to have smaller bodies around and between us. I missed the different scent of my sisters.

I knew this burrow. I used to think it was a

friendly, jolly place. Now it felt strange. Spooky.

Kebiro and Mathani fell asleep fast. Side by side. Their hooves lined up and their heads lined up.

They were both massive, now that I thought about it. I lined up beside them. My hooves were level with theirs. My head was level with theirs. I was massive, too.

Three massive boars in a burrow.

Something deep inside told me Mother was right; boars go off and live alone. What we brothers were doing tonight wasn't the way warthogs were supposed to do it.

But this felt good. And right now I couldn't have been more grateful.

CHAPTER SEVEN

The Pack

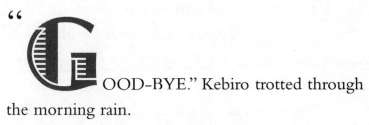

OOD-BYE." Kebiro trotted through the morning rain.

Mathani and I trotted after him.

Kebiro turned on us. "I said, 'Good-bye.'"

Mathani hung his head.

"I thought you were joking," I said. This was not entirely true. Kebiro's tone of voice told me he was dead serious.

"Why would I be joking?"

"We're safer together," said Mathani. "You said that yourself." That was not entirely true, either. We were indeed safer together. But no one had said it, least of all Kebiro.

Kebiro seemed to think hard about this. "Well, all right. You can stay with me, so long as you follow."

Yay.

We trotted to a stream and munched on rushes. A herd of gazelles came along.

Kebiro swung his head toward them. "Perfect."

Several kinds of gazelles roamed the savanna, but I wasn't familiar with these particular ones. They were on the small side, stocky, with boldly patterned coats. A vague worry rose in my chest. "They're not impalas."

"They're gazelles," said Kebiro. "And gazelles are antelopes. Who cares which kind?"

"We've never grazed with ones like them before," grumbled Mathani.

"Do you know, Mathani, all you ever do is complain?" Kebiro glared at Mathani. "That's worse than being a scaredy like Mogo."

Mathani did complain a lot. But this time I

shared his complaint. Even when we were with the sounder, we had never grazed with gazelles like these. That made me feel wary now. It was my duty to stick up for Mathani.

But before I could speak, Mathani said, "I am not worse than Mogo. No one is worse than Mogo."

On second thought, I wouldn't stick up for Mathani.

"See those horns?" said Kebiro. "They're shorter than most gazelle horns."

His point was obvious. Those puny horns made the gazelles look defenseless. Any predator in his right mind would target them over us. It was another case of Look Big—my new credo, thanks to the rhino. Kebiro was smarter than I thought. "You're right, Kebiro."

"See, Mathani? Pull yourself together, boar." Kebiro led us into the herd.

We grazed with the gazelles, staying near the center. I missed the rest of our sounder. But today wasn't turning out so bad.

We gobbled leisurely for a long while. Too leisurely, I realized at last. The day was passing. And darkness could come swiftly and brutally. We had learned that the night before.

"When are we going to find an abandoned aardvark burrow to dig out and make comfortable?" I asked.

"We aren't," said Kebiro.

"What?" I squeaked.

"The sows of our sounder and of the other sounders in our clan have already prepared lots of burrows," said Kebiro. "Why should we go through work for nothing?"

"Good thinking," said Mathani. "See? I don't always complain."

"I suppose not," said Kebiro. "Okay, leave the burrow problem to me. Leave everything to me."

"Of course," said Mathani.

I didn't like this new chumminess between my brothers. It made me feel left out. Besides, what they were saying worried me. But if I protested, they'd just unite against me. I quashed my misgivings and tried to look agreeable.

Slowly the sun lowered. But we kept foraging with the herd.

A gazelle jerked up her head. "Did you see something?"

"No."

"Yes!"

"Oh, no!"

"Wild dogs!"

I looked around frantically. Where? There!

Instantly the gazelles went crazy, their eyes terror-stricken. They stampeded.

We brothers ran with them, flat out.

It was a good thing we had stayed toward the center of the herd, because it turned out that both gazelles and wild dogs ran faster than us. We ran and ran and ran, but we kept falling back toward those dogs.

Time was on our side, though. If the dogs didn't make a kill soon, they would stop.

We ran in a giant circle on the savanna.

And still the dogs chased.

What was going on? Any lioness would have quit by now. But not these dogs.

We ran.

My breath barely came anymore.

I looked back. The lead dog's tongue hung out.

He flagged. But, oh, now another dog took the lead. What? When a leader falls back, the others should fall back, too. What was the matter with these dogs?

We ran. Longer than I'd ever run before. The gazelles circled and zigzagged, and we circled and zigzagged, losing ground every minute. We pigs were at the very rear of the herd now.

I looked over my shoulder again. A big male

dog was behind me. Big—no, he was giant. A head
taller than the others. His eyes glittered with
hunger. And they were on me. I could almost feel
his jaws close on my tail. I could almost smell that
rank breath. The end was near.

When, finally, an exhausted buck to my right
lagged. As one, the dogs changed tack and worked
together to bring down that buck.

The rest of the gazelle herd leaped away and

gradually slowed down.

But we pigs ran and ran.

We came to a burrow and Mathani plunged in.

I plunged in behind him, only to find his rump pushing me back out, straight into Kebiro.

The sow who forced us out now stood at the mouth of the burrow tunnel and thrust her lower tusks forward. "What are you doing? You should be ashamed, big boars like you, trying to take over a family burrow."

"We were chased," said Kebiro.

"By wild dogs," said Mathani.

"Till they took down a gazelle," I said.

"What are you, idiots?" She glared. "I heard the stampede. Thomson's gazelles. Warthogs don't graze with Thomson's gazelles. They're the favorite prey of wild dogs. And Thomson's gazelles are fast, second only to the cheetah. It's dumb to graze with them. It's a miracle the dogs didn't get you."

"We're not dumb," said Kebiro.

Mathani and I stayed silent.

"I recognize you three," said the sow. "You're from a sounder in our clan. I bet your mother just kicked you out, right?"

"Right," said Kebiro.

"Well, go make your own burrows," said the sow. "These family burrows are exactly that—family burrows. Go on, get out of here."

"We've got nowhere to go," said Mathani.

"Whose fault is that? Grow up. Act responsible. And in the meantime, get out of here, you lazy bums."

We trotted away, silenced by worry.

A star twinkled. Now a second one shined beside it. I hated stars. Ugly things. Stars meant it was way too late for warthogs to be out. Side by side those two stars twinkled like eyes. Like the eyes of that giant wild dog.

I saw him in my head. Black circled his eyes. And a black stripe ran down his forehead and spread wide over his muzzle, higher on the right side. It gave him an unbalanced look. He was close behind me—so close. His teeth shined wet. He salivated, already tasting me.

My stomach turned, like it did when I first saw the dog pack. A nauseating mottled wave of brown, black, beige, and white, on long legs with big, round ears. The dogs stood as tall as us, but they were slight—maybe half our weight. One on one, we could probably have held our own against them. But an encounter with wild dogs would never be one on one. They traveled together. And this pack was huge. Who had ever heard of such an enormous pack?

And the way they behaved . . . Yikes. They didn't stalk. They didn't ambush. They didn't even come from downwind. Nothing like lions. They simply loped silently through the grasses, with no attempt to hide. That fact alone was enough to terrorize me; these were totally confident hunters.

Mother had told us wild dogs hunt early in the morning and around dusk. Warthogs rose later and retired earlier, so our paths didn't typically cross.

But here we were, Kebiro and Mathani and me, trotting along in the evening in search of an empty burrow, with a gigantic dog pack somewhere close by.

A thought scrabbled around at the back of my mind. Kebiro was the one who had said we didn't need to make our own burrow.

Maybe it wasn't a good idea to follow Kebiro, after all.

Oh, dear. We were in danger if we stayed together. And we were in danger if we parted.

This conundrum tied my insides in knots.

CHAPTER EIGHT

Lost

"WE NEED an abandoned aardvark burrow," said Mathani.

"Brilliant." Kebiro stamped. "You're just brilliant, Mathani. How are we supposed to know which ones are abandoned and which ones are inhabited?"

Mathani looked at Kebiro.

"The abandoned ones won't smell like aardvarks," I said. "And if they don't smell like warthogs, either, they're free for the taking."

"Do you know what an aardvark smells like?" asked Kebiro.

Oops. None of us did. Aardvarks were nocturnal. We had never come across any.

"Listen to that silence." Kebiro stamped again. "Neither of you can answer. You know what that means?"

"What?" asked Mathani.

"You're both dumb."

That was mean. But I knew Kebiro said it only because he was still smarting from when the sow called us dumb.

We passed a couple of burrow entrances that smelled strongly of warthog. Kebiro didn't pause.

A huge eagle owl swooped down ahead of us and flew off with a hare in her talons. The whole thing happened in seconds. Silently. Like how those wild dogs attacked.

We closed ranks and trotted faster. Night threatened. More stars showed.

We came to a burrow entrance that didn't smell of warthog. It had an odor all right, but unfamiliar and sort of sweet. We stood at a distance.

"Warthogs aren't the only creatures to use abandoned aardvark burrows," said Kebiro. His tone was a demand.

"Civets, hyenas, and jackals," listed Mathani, accommodatingly. "Tree monitors, porcupines, yellow-winged bats, hares, and mongooses." Mother told us that list long ago. I was surprised Mathani remembered it so well. I was the one who usually memorized such things.

"This doesn't smell like civets, hyenas, or jackals," said Kebiro. "And they're the only ones on the list that matter."

"Bats matter," I squealed.

"How?" asked Kebiro. "They eat insects, dirt brain. They would never eat us."

Once, long before, I had run into the far corner of a burrow and come face to face with a bat. He chased me back up the tunnel and then flew over my head so close I felt a wing flap on my ear. I stared as the bright yellow-orange wing membranes disappeared over a small hummock. It gave me the creeps just to remember. "I don't like bats," I said.

"Bah!" said Kebiro. "Does everything in the

world scare you, Mogo? Listen, whatever lives in this burrow, we can chase him out."

"A monitor can bite hard," said Mathani. "A porcupine can stab hard."

Good old Mathani. Back to his complaining. I liked him better that way.

"All right, all right," said Kebiro. "But they won't attack unless we attack first. So if it's a monitor or a porcupine, we'll just go away."

"What if it's an aardvark?" asked Mathani.

Good point. Mother said to find an abandoned burrow, not to kick aardvarks out of their own burrow. She must have had a reason.

"Hmmm." Kebiro backed up more.

Mathani and I backed up, too.

We waited hidden in the deep shadows, our eyes on that burrow.

Moments later a long snout poked out of the entrance. Then a narrow head emerged, attached to a short neck, with long, tubular, upright ears. The squat animal stepped forward, until it was almost completely out in the open. In the faint moonlight it was hard to be entirely sure, but I think it was a dull brown-gray, with only a little hair. Both those things were good, of course. But its back was arched. And, yuck, its front legs were shorter than the hind ones, so it looked like it was headed downhill. The unfortunate thing.

It stood almost as tall as us, though it was much slighter. The three of us could scare it off. But now I noticed: its forefeet had massive, thick claws. This had to be an aardvark; those forefeet were meant for digging. If this aardvark was a fighter, it could hurt us bad.

A strong scent flavored the air. I sniffed hard: milk. This was a nursing mother. Well, that settled it. Any decent mother would fight for her young with whatever weapon she had. And this aardvark had serious weapons.

The aardvark stood motionless. Then she made sudden, giant jumps away from the burrow, into the brush not far from us.

I was so surprised, I practically gagged.

She stopped, rose tall on her hind legs, shot those ears up even higher, and turned her head in all directions. She spotted us instantly and dropped a load of dung.

Whoa. We had never had that effect on a creature before.

I widened my stance to prepare for her attack.

But already her interest had passed. Her head turned this way and that. Well, of course; her caution was for night predators, not night pigs. She listened a long time. Then she covered her dung with dirt.

What a funny, fastidious creature.

She made a few more leaps, stopped, raised up high, and listened again. Finally, she settled into a trot and left. Her muscular tail wiggled like a snake. It tapered to a point that dragged in the dirt.

"Did you see those claws?" said Mathani. "I'm not going down that tunnel."

"No one is," said Kebiro.

We wandered behind the aardvark at a good distance. I wasn't sure why. It was night. We didn't belong out here. Who cared where she was going?

I stayed in line, though. I wasn't about to declare my independence now, at night, out in the open.

The aardvark went straight to a termite mound and dismantled it with her fearsome claws. Then she jammed her long tongue in and pulled it out covered with termites. She moved to a second mound, sturdier than the first. This time she pressed her snout against an opening and made a loud sucking noise. I imagined termites whooshing up her nostrils and down her short throat. After that she sniffed the ground and snuffled up columns of termites that ran along the dirt.

At one point she seemed to figure out that we were following her, not just happening to go the same way. She looked hard at us. Then she lay on her back with all four feet in the air and waved her claws. "Come at me and I'll rip you to shreds," she snarled. "Thin, bloody strips of flesh that not even your mother would recognize."

She had a way with words, all right.

The night sky was black now. A half moon glowed. Stars dazzled.

"I'm tired," groaned Mathani.

We decided to push in under a bush, our rumps together, our tusks facing outward.

"I can't sleep standing up," groaned Mathani.

We got down on our front wrists, then settled onto our haunches.

"It's more comfortable sleeping on our sides," groaned Mathani.

"Enough already," snapped Kibiro. "We're staying exactly as we are. This way we can get to our feet faster if attacked."

Mathani closed his eyes.

Kebiro closed his eyes.

I stared into the black air.

Squeaks and rustles and roars and stamps and slippy-slidey noises filled the night. I pressed my rump harder against Mathani's and Kebiro's.

We were lost. Three little pigs. Lost.

Mother said to find an abandoned aardvark burrow, as though it was something easy.

It wasn't easy.

And that mean old sow told us to grow up and act responsible. As though that was easy, too.

It wasn't.

Nothing was easy.

CHAPTER NINE

The Ratel Burrow

ORNING came early. Sleeping outside like that, we had nothing to shield our faces from the sunshine.

I woke quickly, barely rested. I checked on my brothers. They looked back at me groggily. Not a promising way to start the day.

But we had to. And fast. There was no time to lose. I had made a resolution last night. I had to speak up before I lost my nerve.

"I'm going to find a burrow," I announced. "An abandoned aardvark burrow. I'm going to widen it so that it's comfortable." I couldn't tell how Kebiro was taking this news. His face was blank. The possibility loomed large that he'd charge me. I swayed on unsteady legs. "If you two want to come, that would be good."

Mathani and Kebiro just stood there.

"I'd like that a lot," I said. "You're my brothers. I want to be with you."

Mathani and Kebiro just stood there.

I trotted away slowly. Then I stopped and looked over my shoulder. "Yup, I sure do want you with me. You're my brothers. Yup."

Mathani came after me.

Kebiro watched. All at once he burst forth and went to the front of the line. "Finding a burrow is the first order of the day. Exactly my idea."

I gratefully assumed last position in line.

We found three burrows right off. All of them had fresh scents: warthogs, warthogs, and aardvarks. Well, that was okay. We had plenty of time.

And, yes yes yes, the fourth burrow was the treasure. No recent smells at all.

"This time, me first," said Kebiro. He pushed through the entrance. And stopped. His rump sealed up the top of the opening. "Help," we heard distantly. Kebiro was caught in the tunnel.

Mathani and I looked at each other. This was a totally new problem.

"Help," called Kebiro.

"Do you want to go in or out?" called back Mathani.

"Out," called Kebiro.

That was an unfortunate request. Warthogs could push easily. But how could we pull? And what would we pull?

Mathani and I got the same idea at once.

"You or me?" I asked.

"You," said Mathani.

"You have to promise not to tell him who did it," I said.

"I promise."

I clamped my jaws on Kebiro's tail and pulled and tugged.

At last he wriggled free and I had just enough time to back out of the way before he spun around and glowered at us.

"That aardvark must have been skinny," said Mathani.

Kebiro trembled with disgust. "It's awful to be stuck."

We gave snorts of sympathy.

"Well, I'm not digging this burrow out," said Kebiro. "The tunnel goes down sharply. It's deep. So the ground is really hard, even after all this rain. It would take a whole day just to widen the tunnel, and then I bet the chamber inside wouldn't hold more than one of us, anyway. To make the chamber big enough would take a week. Let's find another."

"Right," said Mathani.

"Right," I said.

"I'm hungry," said Mathani.

"Soon," said Kebiro. "Soon."

A small, drab olive bird flew past. I recognized it immediately from the white wedge in the tail feathers: a honeyguide. The bird called out, then zoomed down toward a stand of acacia trees, covered with white blossoms and surrounded by low thickets. He looped upward at the last moment. He swooped from tree to tree, calling repeatedly.

We knew exactly what was going on; the bird

was alerting a ratel—a honey badger—to the location of honeybee nests.

And there was a ratel, emerging from a burrow right on cue. He came out walking almost level, so that burrow had to be really shallow. A short guy, he stood only as tall as our legs, but the sight of him made me gasp. His neck and shoulders exuded strength. Even his thick head seemed ferocious. And the enormous claws on his forelegs rivaled those of the aardvark. A white fur mantle ran from his head down his back to the tip of his tail. His underside and legs were black. A striking fellow.

"Let's follow him," said Kebiro.

I hesitated. "I don't know about those acacias." I didn't have to say more. We all knew lions liked to hide in thickets like those.

"All right. We can watch from here."

We huddled together.

With a quick glance the ratel noted us, then dismissed us. He let out a guttural growl. The bird called back. The ratel lumbered after the birdcall, growling intermittently. He had a funny, bow-legged gait.

A breeze rose and carried the delicate perfume

of the acacia blossoms to us. We sniffed deeply. No lion scent.

In silent agreement we walked after the ratel.

But what was that?

A wild dog appeared. A giant of a dog. With a black swath down his face, across his muzzle, around both eyes. Higher on the right side.

I gulped in recognition.

The monster dog was alone this time. He glanced my way. As our eyes met, I could see the truth: he'd never dare come after a full-grown warthog. Or never after three full-grown warthogs.

I moved closer to Mathani.

The monster dog turned his attention back to the ratel. He had a surprised look on his face, as though he had only been out wandering and didn't expect to come across food. But his expression changed fast; that ratel was an easy meal. The monster ran right at it.

But the ratel did the craziest thing; he faced the monster. He growled like a fiend. Fearless.

The monster dog went straight for the ratel's throat. His teeth closed over the fur. But the ratel's skin was loose and thick, and that monster slipped right off, and clamped his jaws around the ratel's hind leg, instead.

In an instant, the ratel swiped at the groin of the monster, who yelped and twisted away just in time. His claws barely nicked the monster's hind paw.

The monster whimpered and ran off.

We were stunned at such a display of courage, and even more stunned that the little guy won.

The ratel lifted his head and growled.

The honeyguide called back.

And that ratel galloped off, clumsily, toward the acacias. His left hind leg was clearly injured. Blood matted his fur. But nothing was going to keep him from that honey. I suddenly loved him for that stubborness. Mother called us stubborn. This little ratel was just like us.

We followed, fascinated.

The ratel sniffed around the thicket. He located the beehive. Then he let out a stink.

What was that about? We moved away from the smelly cloud.

So did the honeybees. They abandoned that hive so fast, you'd have thought it was swarming time.

The ratel rubbed his backside around the hive. A few more bees fled. If there were any left inside, they had to be dead by now; it was a killer stink.

The ratel bit the hive in two, then he scooped out the honeycomb.

All this while, the honeyguide waited in the highest tree. When the ratel finished, it would be the bird's turn. He would eat what was left of the honeycomb, and any dead bees lying around. So both animals would win—the ratel and the bird. It was a superb arrangement. We watched, looking forward to the end of the show.

That was when we heard the buzz. Louder and louder. I looked around.

The bees had returned. They circled the ratel's head. They dove at him, looking for somewhere to sting through that bristly hair. And they found it: the ratel's wounded hind leg. They stung and stung and stung. The ratel swiped at them futilely. He growled. Bees flew into his open mouth and stung his tongue. Bees stung the skin that covered his earholes. Bees stung his small, startled eyes.

His growls stopped. He flopped on his side. He didn't move again.

The bees had won.

All because of the open wound, the injury the monster dog inflicted.

We stared.

The honeyguide flew away.

Kebiro was the first to shake free of the horror. He trotted back toward where the ratel had come from.

Mathani and I trotted after him.

"What are you doing?" asked Mathani.

"Opportunity," said Kebiro. He stopped in front of the ratel's burrow. "This is my new home."

"What if there's someone in there?" I squealed.

"There isn't. He was a mature male. I bet

his rotten mother kicked him out, just like ours did."

I wasn't happy at hearing our mother called rotten. But I didn't want a fight. "It's got to be too small."

"I can widen it big enough for me," said Kebiro.

For him? Only for him? I held back a squeak.

"I thought you didn't want to go through all that work," said Mathani.

"It'll be easy," said Kebiro. "It's obviously a shallow burrow. So the dirt will be soft." He stuck his snout in the entrance and dug around, tossing out dirt. "See?" he called over his shoulder. "Easy." He dug away.

"Mother always led us to deep burrows," I said.

"Mother isn't here," said Kebiro. "In case you didn't notice."

"I'm hungry," said Mathani.

"Later," called Kebiro. His head was completely submerged in the tunnel now. "When I finish, we can go eat something."

I looked at Mathani sadly. "He's making a home only he can fit in."

"Worse," said Mathani. "He wants us to wait while he does it. And we haven't eaten all day." He gave a little sob. "Kebiro is bad. And it was your idea to find a burrow first thing, when we always eat first thing. You're bad, too."

"I'm just trying to be sensible."

"You're failing," said Mathani.

He was right. Hunger hurt. This had been a horrible day so far. "Let's go find a close spot to graze."

"Good," said Mathani.

Just then my snout twitched. Mathani's snout twitched. We had caught the odor at the same time. In an instant we were digging furiously around the entrance to the ratel burrow. I uncovered a dead bird. Mathani uncovered a dead lizard. We ate the carrion. Waste not, want not, after all. That was a warthog saying. Then we snuffled along and uncovered more dead animals. Frogs and toads. Rodents of all sizes. Even a snake.

"This ratel must have been a hoarder," I said. "Saving up for rough times ahead."

Mathani swallowed the last of the snake. "You're not as bad as I said." He burped.

I moved closer.

We chewed more slowly now.

"You're actually good." Mathani swallowed a mouse. "And we do need a burrow. You are sensible."

I moved closer still.

Well past the middle of the day, Kebiro emerged. "You should see the sleeping chamber. It's lined with leaves. Soft as a sow belly. That ratel knew how to live, all right."

"Okay," I said.

"Okay, what?" said Kebiro.

"I want to see it." The only burrows I had ever been in were dug by aardvarks. A ratel burrow was new. "Step aside."

Kebiro looked taken aback. "What's gotten into you?"

"You offered," I said.

"That's right," said Mathani. "I heard you."

"Well, okay. But come out quick. It's my home, not yours."

I went into the burrow. It gave me the jitters. I came out. "It's shallow."

"Do you have to keep griping about that?" Kebiro stamped. "You know what? You're jealous because I got such a nice home with so little work."

"There's no back door," I said. "No way to escape."

"Who needs a back door? Nothing follows a warthog into his burrow," said Kebiro. "Stop being a worrywart. A worry warthog, I mean. Ha! Did you get that?"

I didn't answer.

"Let's go eat," said Kebiro. "The afternoon is already passing. I'm starving."

Mathani and I looked at each other. Our tummies were already full. And we didn't have burrows for the night. But splitting up before we had to was more than we could face. We followed Kebiro.

CHAPTER TEN

The Mongoose Burrow

"WELL, look at these," said Kebiro, only minutes later. "This is our lucky day."

A zillion paw prints made a crazy pattern ahead of us. Five toes on the forefeet, all clawed; five toes on the hind feet. And only the claw of the first toe of each hind foot showed in the dirt— well behind the other four toes. No doubt about it, a troop of banded mongooses. And they were traveling slowly, or they would have retracted their claws. This was a satisfied, happy troop.

Kebiro cantered now. Mathani and I followed, into the tall brush.

Soon those little grayish-brown guys sprawled out in front of us. Everywhere I looked—huge bushy tails and coarse fur with light-and-dark vertical bands across the back and flanks. Maybe forty of them. Maybe fifty. They scratched around, moving in a zigzag on elegant dark legs, eating beetles and spiders and whatever else came scurrying out of the grasses to escape their claws, singing, "Yum, yum, yum."

The sentry mongoose stood on his hind legs and looked hard at us. But he didn't let out a warning call. Warthogs were neither threat nor stranger.

We went right into the center of the troop. They gave us wide berth.

Kebiro foraged immediately.

Mathani and I weren't

hungry, naturally. We dropped onto our wrists and waited.

Soon enough the mongooses approached. I closed my eyes and savored a moment of glorious anticipation. And, yup, now I felt a cold nose. And another. Those triangular heads with pointed faces were poking all over me. Their claws combed through my mane.

"Yum, yum." *Crunch crunch.* Mongooses were eating the ticks off my back.

Oh, I loved this. I loved everything about it. Why, come to think of it, the friendship that often forms between a troop of mongooses and a sounder of warthogs was as good as that between a honeyguide and a ratel. "I could stay here forever," I said. "Surrounded by warm bodies, getting groomed."

"You like these scratchy little things?" asked Mathani. "The only good part is knowing the sentry will call a warning if danger approaches."

The sentry. Yes. That made it all even better. We could actually relax.

When I opened my eyes, the sun was setting. The day had gone by too fast. The female mongooses moved in a single direction now, their flat, broad ears alert. Their gait changed to a waddle because their mammary glands had filled up with milk.

I saw termite mounds not far off—that's where their burrows were, of course. And undoubtedly little ones were waiting for their mothers.

Mothers and babies, together.

A pang of envy made me swallow hard. The males clustered around the females. The troop moved as a unit. Homeward.

I jumped to my hooves.

Mathani jumped up, too.

Where was Kebiro?

Ah, there, at the edge of the mongoose troop. He plowed through the dirt and ate lazily. Not a care in the world. After all, he had somewhere to sleep come nightfall.

We didn't.

The mongoose sentry let off a loud, sharp alarm call. I winced and swung around, looking every which way. Over the little slope beyond Kebiro, wild dogs came trotting. Lots of them.

Every wild dog had unique markings.

Everyone knew that. So there was no mistaking him: the monster dog was in the lead. It was that same enormous pack that had attacked the herd of Thomson's gazelles the day before.

The mongooses ran like crazy for the termite mounds.

Kebiro ran for his ratel burrow.

Mathani and I had nowhere to run. We stood like dolts for a split second. Then we ran after the mongooses.

The mongooses dove into holes in the sides of the termite mounds.

Mathani and I circled the mounds, looking for a hole large enough to dive into. They were half as big as we needed. In desperation I jumped on the ground between two holes, until it collapsed, forming one tunnel that was almost wide enough. Mathani did the same. We wriggled our rumps down inside. We swung our tusks out threateningly at the world.

We waited, mostly exposed, completely terrified. Not a single mongoose remained out in the open. The dogs would come and attack Mathani and me from all sides. We had no chance.

We waited.

Yips and yowls came to us from beyond the thickets, behind the small hummocks, ever more distant.

That was the direction of Kebiro's ratel burrow.

My heart missed a beat.

"Kebiro is a fast pig," I said to Mathani.

"Right," said Mathani. "I bet he got home in time."

"Right," I said back. "What do you make of those dogs? They're hunting two days in a row. Lions don't do that."

"Maybe wild dogs hunt every day," said Mathani.

"With a pack that big," I said, "they might have to."

"Or maybe it's just the way they're made. We eat every day. Could be they do, too."

The yips were so distant we could hardly hear them now.

Mathani was the first to scrabble his rump free of the hole. He turned around and dug madly with his wide snout.

That was the right thing to do, of course. Once

the dog pack realized they couldn't get at Kebiro, they would head back this way. Hungry, vicious dogs. With that monster in the lead.

I dug like a maniac. This termite mound was fairly tough stuff. Aadrvarks, ratels, mongooses, they all had great digging claws. The only thing a warthog could dig with was his snout.

Other parts of us were strong, though. I kicked. The sides of the tunnel crumbled. Between my hooves and snout, I soon found myself inside a burrow.

It was dark in here.

And I wasn't alone. The strong smell of mongoose made my nose swell. I sneezed.

"Is that you, Mogo?" called Mathani.

"Wow. We're in the same burrow," I called back.

"Half the colony is in here," called Mathani. "It seems the tunnels all lead to one giant burrow. What a stinky crowd. I'm coming to find you."

I strained to see. There were mothers and nursing babies everywhere.

"Watch where you step," I called. "You don't want to trample the little ones."

"They're not that little," called Mathani.

It was true. Those squirming, tumbling babies were almost half the size of their mothers. But even if they were big in a mongoose sense, they were little compared to a warthog.

"They're little enough," I called. "Stop. There's no way you can get to me."

"You mean I have to sleep surrounded by them?"

"Just for tonight. See you in the morning." I felt around with my snout till I was sure the ground under me was clear. I slowly lowered myself to my belly. And finally, I stretched out on my side.

I missed Mathani, even though I knew he was within calling distance.

And I missed Kebiro. Was he sleeping peacefully in his own burrow? Or was he missing us, too?

A mongoose crawled over my back and down. Then it turned around and crawled on top of me again. A young one. He plucked a tick off me and crunched it up. Then he gave a little groan, said, "Yum," sat down, and fell asleep. I didn't feel him topple over. Was he going to sleep sitting up all night?

But who cared? The important point was: he was sleeping on me. My siblings had slept on top of me before. Many times. Their weight was always reassuring. This was different. This little mongoose was just a spot of warmth on my side, but it was still comforting.

I closed my eyes.

Another mongoose crawled on top of me and sat beside the first one. Then another. They ate ticks, said, "Yum," and fell asleep.

This was getting better all the time.

CHAPTER ELEVEN

The Aardvark Burrow

THE MONGOOSES left the burrow, and it was still really early in the morning—earlier than warthogs rose. I felt disoriented as the faint sunlight crept down the shaft of the tunnel I had widened— the one that had originally been two. I could see a little better now. The babies, who had purred when they were nursing, now rolled into a silent pile and fell back asleep.

I followed the adults and peeked cautiously out the hole.

Most of the troop was already zigzagging far away. But a small group of females foraged close to the burrow. Much closer than the afternoon before. That felt ominous. My nerves jangled.

"Hey?" I called. "Do you think those wild dogs will return?"

At my words, the females stood at attention, tall on their hind feet, and jerked their faces toward me.

"The dogs," I said. "Remember?"

"Eh," said one at last. "Wild dogs change territory every day."

They went back to foraging.

I stepped out and paced in front of my burrow entrance. If wild dogs changed territory every day, why had we seen this pack two days in a row?

Mathani peeked out of a nearby hole.

I raced to greet him. We bumped heads.

He joined me pacing for a while. Then he chewed a spike of grass and pretty soon he was off grazing.

I watched him enviously. I was hungry, too. How far did I dare stray from this burrow?

A mother mongoose zipped past me down the tunnel.

I tensed up, ready to dive down my hole.

But no one else followed her. No one else seemed to even notice.

She emerged moments later with dozens of youngster mongooses in tow. They scampered around, jumping in surprise at grasshoppers. Oh, I got it. The little group of adult females was watching over the babies for the whole troop. Mongooses had communal child care, just like warthogs. Nice.

I watched the mongoose mothers. Not a one of them gave any sign of being worried. Not even with the babies exposed like that. They were alert—but not anxious. And the young blithely ate insects. "Yum, yum, yum."

They clearly believed the dogs were far away.

Maybe Kebiro was right. I shouldn't be such a worry warthog. I wandered over to join Mathani and eat beside him. Brothers together.

But I didn't have much appetite, after all. Now that I had thought about Kebiro, I couldn't get him out of my head.

I nudged Mathani. "Want to look for Kebiro?"

"Sure."

We stood there, awkwardly.

Without Kebiro, who should lead?

Mathani blinked and took off toward the ratel burrow. I followed.

The morning was clean and bright. It had rained during the night, and sunlight glinted off beads of water everywhere.

A flash of blue and pink caught my eye. A lilac-breasted roller. The glorious bird landed high on an acacia tree in the very stand where the bees had killed the ratel.

A tail hung from a lower branch. A long furry tail.

My heart clutched. But it wasn't a cheetah tail this time. It was a lone olive baboon.

"Look, Mathani," I said. "An olive baboon."

"Just one?" Mathani stopped and we both looked. "Dead baboon." He trotted on.

The baboon was not dead, really. But I knew what Mathani meant. Once, when we were small, our sounder came across a dead baboon. He looked strong and young. There were no signs that other baboons had been in the area. And no evidence of what had killed him. My aunt said it was because

121

he'd gone off alone. "A lone baboon is a dead baboon," she said. And she turned the occasion into a lesson: "Just like a lone piglet is a dead piglet."

That baboon in the acacia tree now looked plenty strong, at least from this distance. Large and thick. The hair around the shoulders and neck was a bit longer, forming a mantle, so I knew this was a male. I could have guessed from his bulk anyway. A female would have been half that size.

His face in profile was long, ending in a black muzzle. It was strikingly like a dog's. And even more powerful. My insides shook.

The baboon shifted and looked at us. I couldn't smell him from here. There was no wind. And I couldn't see his eyes, they were so close set and deep under that prominent forehead. But I could feel in my bones that he smelled us. It was our smell that made him turn his head. And I could feel him looking right into my eyes.

"Wahoo," he called.

I had no idea what that meant. Maybe it was a special word only baboons used. In any case, it didn't sound hostile. It sounded lonely.

I trotted fast to catch up to Mathani. Kebiro's ratel burrow wasn't too far now.

The closer we got, the shorter my breath got. Foreboding filled me.

We stopped a good distance away. The ratel burrow had been dug open. Tracks littered the area—those hideous, four-toed, long-nailed tracks. There was no sign of Kebiro. Only the smell of death in the air.

"I hate wild dogs," said Mathani.

"Me, too."

Mathani turned back toward the way we had come.

"Where are you going?" I asked.

"I'm sticking with the mongooses."

"But we need . . ."

Mathani stamped his front hooves. "Don't always make trouble, Mogo. Our mongoose burrow is deeper than that ratel burrow."

"It isn't as deep as an aardvark burrow," I said. "Look what happened to. . ." I couldn't bring myself to say our brother's name. "You know."

Mathani turned in a circle. Then he turned again. Then he turned once more. "You and I already dug two tunnels. That was hard work. We already have a burrow. With mongoose sentries. Only a fool would turn that down."

"Mother said . . ."

"Mother isn't here," said Mathani. "In case you didn't notice."

That smarted. I stamped my front hooves.

Mathani turned halfway, so he faced me broadside. Like Kebiro did that time. Dominance was clear: Mathani was now in charge.

He trotted back toward the mongooses.

My heart longed to trot after him. The last thing I wanted was to be left alone. But my head told me the mongoose burrows weren't right. Not for us.

"We can work together," I called. "Remember that abandoned aardvark burrow two days ago? It isn't far. We can widen it together. We can share a home."

Mathani didn't even look back over his shoulder. But he called, "Warthogs aren't cut out for digging, Mogo. Join me when you realize that."

I watched him leave.

Suddenly I felt small, naked, defenseless.

I had never been alone like this.

A lone piglet was a dead piglet.

I knew I wasn't a piglet. But in this moment, I felt like one.

Panic threatened.

But I knew what to do.

I galloped the whole way to the abandoned aardvark burrow that Kebiro had gotten stuck in, the one I had pulled him out of.

It was still uninhabited.

If I got stuck in that tunnel, there would be no one to pull me out.

Stop it! That kind of thinking wouldn't help.

I stamped. I dug. I kicked. I slashed at the tunnel walls with my tusks. I worked all morning. I was hungry and exhausted. But I dug like my life depended on it. I dug all afternoon. I dug all evening.

Finally I made it down to the very bottom of the tunnel, only to find that Kebiro had been right: the chamber was small. Given the extra length my tusks added to my overall size, there was no room to turn around. If I entered headfirst, I'd have to exit rumpfirst.

Well, then, I'd have to be sure to always enter rumpfirst. That was how the last warthog was supposed to enter anyway.

And for now I was the last warthog. And the first warthog.

The only warthog.

I backed out, hoping no nocturnal predator lay waiting for my tasty flanks.

Then I turned around and backed in again.

I settled on my haunches. There was no room to lie on my side.

Tomorrow I could work on widening the chamber.

But, no, tomorrow I would eat. I had gone a whole day with almost no food. I had to regain my strength. I could widen the chamber two days from now.

That was a sensible plan. The kind of plan a lone warthog should make.

I remembered the lone baboons. The one who died. And the one in the acacia tree this morning. Was he still alive?

I swallowed the lump in my throat.

CHAPTER TWELVE

Dogs Again

I WOKE EARLY and climbed up my tunnel. It was damp near the opening. I peeked out.

Rain splashed in. It came down hard and fast.

I opened my mouth and gulped greedily.

I couldn't smell predators in the rain. I should have backed into the chamber again and waited for it to stop. But hunger pressed me onward.

And I missed my brothers.

No, I missed my brother Mathani.

Kebiro was probably dead.

For a moment I couldn't hear anything. It was as though my ears were pinned shut. Sadness made me so woozy, I dropped to my wrists.

Poor Kebiro.

But Mathani was safe in the mongoose burrow. Even if we parted at night, there was no reason why we couldn't spend our days together.

I trotted through the pounding rain. I couldn't wait to see Mathani. I cantered now. I galloped.

In my blind rush I almost collided with a baboon. He was fiddling in the mud, both hands busy, and he didn't bother to get out of the way. I swerved at the last moment and tumbled down an incline.

Full-grown warthogs did not roll easily. I stood up, bruised and battered, and amazed all my limbs were still solid.

The baboon looked down at me. There were no others with him. It had to be the same lone male from the night before.

He rose onto all fours and stood sideways, displaying his full size. He turned his head and stared down at me. His purplish rump was big and callused. His tail stood up erect a little ways, then bent in a crazy angle toward the ground. It looked broken—but I knew that was just how baboon tails were. He closed his eyes, showing white eyelids, and opened his enormous mouth, showing long white canines. There was no mistake about it—those teeth could do damage. Then he snapped his jaw shut and hurled something at me.

I squealed and jumped back. It landed with a

slap in front of me, splashing mud on my snout. I sniffed. A big, fat, yellow, curled mushroom. With a bite taken out of it.

I looked at the baboon.

"Wahoo," he said.

I couldn't fathom why a baboon would throw a mushroom at me. The display of those gigantic fangs made me wary. But the mushroom couldn't be poisonous, not with that bite taken out of it.

I nibbled a corner. It was good. "Thanks," I called.

The baboon sat again and resumed his business: searching in the mud.

I resumed my own business: returning to the termite mound where my brother awaited me. But I went slowly now. No point in risking collisions, after all.

I saw Mathani's head peek out of the hole just about the same moment he saw me. Grunts burst from our throats. We ran toward each other and pressed snouts hard and long. Together again. Hurrah!

The mongooses emerged from the burrow gradually. They wrinkled their noses and twitched their whiskers. "Rain, rain," came the lament from every burrow hole. "Yucky, yucky rain. Rain again."

This morning the babies came out of the burrow with the adults. The troop zigzagged through the rain into the grasses.

Mathani and I followed, but far to the rear. We wanted to be as close as possible to the burrow holes when the troop stopped to eat.

But the troop didn't stop to eat. It raced on and on through the delicious grasses, never pausing. What was going on?

The troop ran through the rain endlessly. When the little ones lagged, the mothers nipped at their heels.

Then they stopped. All of them. At a giant termite mound. The adults went to work digging. They ate termites in the process. The babies clustered in the grasses and slurped up insects. There was a festive air about the whole thing.

I got it; they were changing homes. In the past every time our sounder had made friends with a mongoose troop, they disappeared after a few days. Mongooses must simply like to be on the go.

From the way they cavorted as they worked, I was sure they'd been looking forward to this particular move for a long time. Probably since the babies were born. At least five or six weeks. No wonder they were practically having a party right now.

A sentry climbed to the top of the mound and kept watch. I didn't know what good he could do. If a predator came, no one had anywhere to hide.

And that included Mathani and me.

The old standby rule came back to me: run and dodge, run and dodge, run and dodge. It was a good rule, so long as the predator chasing you tired out quickly. Like lions.

But the predator that worried me most these days didn't tire out quickly. I closed my eyes and the image of the wild dog pack filled my head.

I turned to Mathani. "The mongooses are making a new home."

"I can see that." Mathani sighed.

"If the wild dogs come . . ."

"They'll go after the mongooses," said Mathani.

I thought of Kebiro running, running. "They didn't last time."

"You're right," said Mathani.

"If you're going to stay with them," I said, "you better get started on your own hole now."

"You can see the problem as well as I can; these guys are nomadic," said Mathani. "If I go through all the work of widening one of their new tunnels, I'll just have to do it all over again the next time they move. I'll spend my life widening tunnels."

He turned in a circle. He turned and turned.

"Stop turning," I said.

Mathani stopped. "I'm a warthog; I'm no digger." He turned once more. "I'm not staying with them."

"Oh, good! You've come to your senses." I was so happy, I wanted to spin around myself. "Let's go find you an abandoned aardvark burrow. Close to mine. We can . . ."

"Forget it," said Mathani. "Didn't you hear me? I despise excavating. I'm never doing it again." His eyes brightened. "And why should I? I already have a good burrow." He trotted quickly back toward the old mongoose burrow.

I trotted behind. "It's not deep," I said.

"It's deep enough. And you can stay with

me, if you want. My burrow is big and empty."

I imagined us stretched out on our sides. Breathing each other's warmth. Brothers together.

The rain slowed to a drizzle by the time Mathani's mongoose burrow was in sight. The rush was over. We stopped and ate.

Finally, Mathani said, "I want a nap. Care to join me?"

A shrill bark came from somewhere high.

Mathani ran for his burrow.

I didn't follow. Something was off about that bark. The wild dogs didn't bark in the past; they attacked silently. Besides, I didn't see any wild dogs. That wasn't like them, either. They didn't hide when they hunted. They came right out in the open and chased.

Another shrill bark from high up again. I looked around. An old fig tree stood to the right. A familiar olive-brown tail hung from it.

"Wait for me, Mathani," I called. He was halfway to the burrow now, going at full speed. "It's not dogs. It's just . . ."

That's when the dogs appeared. Their heads popped up from the many holes of the mongoose burrow. They had taken it over. Mathani was running straight into the jaws of the monster dog!

He spun away at the same moment I did.

We raced for my aardvark burrow.

CHAPTER THIRTEEN

Alone

RACED faster and faster. Home. Home.

I couldn't take the time to back in. Mathani must be close behind me, so he needed me to get out of the way fast.

I plunged in headfirst.

I jammed myself as deep into the chamber as I could, and waited for Mathani's rump to come smack against mine.

Come on, Mathani.

I waited.

Run, Mathani. Run run. Back into the tunnel. Come on!

I waited.

Nothing butted up against me.

This couldn't be happening.

I sank to my wrists. What if he didn't make it?

No, I couldn't bear to think that way. I would just wait.

Wait wait wait wait wait.

I fell asleep waiting.

When I woke, my haunches were stiff. I must have slept all night.

The horror of the day before crept back into my head. Scenes replayed. All those dog ears—tall and wide, black-rimmed. All those dog muzzles— black and long and bloodthirsty. They had come popping out of the mongoose burrow holes, one after another, like a sudden disease.

Who could have known wild dogs liked abandoned mongoose burrows?

They had taken over Mathani's home.

Mathani.

I wiggled my rump.

Nothing wiggled back.

I reversed up the tunnel a little ways.

Nothing.

I returned to the chamber.

Mathani wasn't here.

I wasn't stupid. Mathani had been much closer to the dogs than I had been.

But he was a strong pig. Mathani had to be okay.

And now, against all my wishes, the memory of a sound came. Not a bark or a howl or a yap. But a squeal that had turned into a shriek. A death shriek. It could only have come from Mathani.

Dear Mathani.

I stood there.

Every part of me felt unbearably heavy. I could hardly hold up my head. My wrists threatened to buckle. My lungs wanted to collapse.

My brothers were gone.

I remembered Mother saying that warthogs shouldn't cry. But, like my brothers said, Mother wasn't here.

I cried. I wept.

I was alone in the world for real now. Entirely on my own.

And I was headfirst in my chamber, with no room to turn around.

I didn't know what to do but wait.

Time crawled.

My stomach growled. My mouth grew dry. My eyes burned.

I backed partway up the tunnel. Then I stopped.

There were many ways to die. Being ripped apart by wild dogs might be the worst.

I went forward into the chamber again.

Eventually, I fell asleep.

When I woke, my head buzzed, as though bees had flown in through my ears. I remembered the ratel, overpowered by the bees.

But he'd been brave. He had stood up to the monster dog as though he, the little ratel, was a lion.

I could stand up to a lone wild dog if I had to. I might even be able to keep him at bay. I didn't have tusks for nothing.

It was the hunting pack that scared the wits out of me. A single warthog had no chance against a pack. They sighted their prey and ran it down relentlessly.

That was how they worked.

Oh, right! They didn't sit outside a burrow entrance and wait for the animal to emerge.

That was the lion's way.

So the dog pack was not waiting outside my burrow.

But a lion could be.

Conundrum.

I closed my eyes. It was too dark to see in the chamber anyway. And maybe with my eyes closed I'd fall asleep again.

My stomach twisted in hunger.

If I stayed here, I would undoubtedly die. If I went outside, there was a chance I'd live.

Maybe that was the right way to look at it. The chance to live—an adventure.

Onward, to adventure. Yes, yes, that was the right mindset.

I backed up the tunnel again. One step after another. Up up up.

Adventure. Yes.

Rain hit my rump.

I emerged and spun around to face potential attackers. Lack of food had made me so faint, that single spin dizzied me. I stumbled into the brush and stuffed my mouth. I ripped plants up whole in my haste.

A roar came from the direction of the acacia trees.

I thought of the lone baboon, with his tail hanging down from that tree. I remembered the tail in the fig tree near the mongoose burrow. And the shrill bark. One and then another. Had it really been the baboon?

Was a lion after him now? Lions wouldn't attack a baboon tribe. No animal would. When baboons ganged up together, they could turn any predator into prey. But a lone baboon, that was another story.

Just like a lone warthog.

I gobbled faster and faster. Hunger forced me on.

But I knew this was a bad way to eat. The only sensible thing was to forage by day, in the middle of a herd of zebras or gnus or something else that didn't run faster than me—so that I wouldn't be the easiest target.

Giraffes! Giraffes were speedy in bursts, but not as speedy as warthogs. Plus they could see forever; nothing could sneak up on a giraffe. And, best of all, wild dogs didn't go after giraffe herds. A single giraffe kick could send a dog flying.

This plan, however, broke the Look Big rule. But I couldn't think of anything better. And it was time for me to make my own rules.

At last my stomach relented. I ran back to my burrow, entered rump-first, and shimmied down to the chamber. I was asleep before I even fell to my haunches.

CHAPTER FOURTEEN

That Crazy Baboon
and the Beautiful Sow

EARLY the next morning I started my search for a giraffe herd. This area had several stands of acacias, and giraffes loved acacia leaves, despite the thorns.

First, however, I wanted a good long drink. I headed for the stream, which had turned wide as a river from all the rain.

I was standing with my forelegs in the water, lapping gratefully, when I heard splashes behind me.

I swirled around to face my attacker.

The olive baboon skipped past on his hind legs, across the shallow river. He held his arms out high to both sides, his elbows crooked and his hands hanging from limp wrists. His tail went up and then bent down in that crazy broken look.

I couldn't figure what on earth possessed him to act like that, when, *zip*, a startled mudfish jumped up beside the baboon's leg and he caught it in his hand.

I had never seen anyone catch a fish that way before.

The baboon gave a screech of delight. He bit the head off the fish and looked at me as he chomped. Then he skipped up and down the river. Mudfish jumped all around him, and he swiped wildly at them. But he wasn't lucky enough to catch another.

If that was his method of hunting, he must have gone hungry a lot. I'd never seen such an inefficient predator.

I drank slowly, aware that the baboon was watching me. I looked up to face him.

But he turned and flopped into the water and swam. Swam!

Well, each to his own.

A series of water striders did their spooky thing, racing across the surface of the water. On a whim, I ate a few. They tasted pretty good.

But, on the whole, I preferred vegetation. Some nice acacia leaves, dropped by a browsing giraffe from the very top, where the leaves are most tender—now that would have been heaven. Cheered by the thought of what messy eaters they were, I trotted off in search of giraffes.

And, *whap*, something hit me in the flank.

I let out a startled "oomph" and spun around.

A mudfish flopped on the dirt.

I looked up. The baboon sat on the riverbank, with his rump to me. He glanced over his shoulder casually and gave a lazy half-lidded look, as though the whole world bored him.

Who did he think he was fooling?

The fish gasped its last and lay still. I nosed it. Baboons ate pretty much anything. Warthogs weren't picky eaters, either. Still, I'd never heard of a warthog eating fish.

I took a small bite. Not bad. I ate the whole fish.

This was the second time this baboon had given me a gift. He was an oddball, no doubt about it. But gifts were good. "Thanks," I called.

"Wahoo," called the baboon.

He looked vulnerable, alone, and dripping wet. He was lion meat, for sure.

So was I, standing here like this.

I had a quick impulse to dash for my burrow.

And what was I thinking, looking for a giraffe herd to graze with? I had forgotten all about the plan to widen my burrow chamber. I needed to do that, so if a lioness chased me, I could plunge in headfirst and turn around inside.

Oh, dear. There were just too many things for a piggy to keep in his head.

I trotted into the grasses and ate fast. Then I went home and dug.

It was brutal work. The chamber was deep, so the earth was rock hard. I kicked and scraped and slashed and even bit at those walls. Then I shoveled the dirt up the tunnel and out.

By nightfall my chamber was big. I went in headfirst, turned around inside, and went right back out headfirst. I snorted my delight.

"Wahoo," came a call from the direction of the acacia stand.

Crazy baboon.

But he wasn't lion meat yet. He was still alive.

So was I.

We were alike—two loners who never should have been on their own.

All at once I had to swallow the longing that filled my throat. I wanted that baboon to stay alive. I wanted him to have a good, long, happy life. I wanted it so much.

I shuffled down the tunnel and slept, sprawled on my side, as safe as a lone pig could be.

The next morning it was finally giraffe time.

There had been a heavy downpour at dawn, then it ceased, just like that. Sun sparkled off the puddles on all sides. It was a good day for an adventure. A good day to be alive.

I trotted along, looking carefully at each stand of trees. Giraffes could blend easily, after all. It was hard to see them if they weren't moving.

That's when I spotted a sounder. This wasn't my sounder, but it must have been part of the larger clan that my sounder belonged to.

There were four sows. One had a long scar across her rump. A close encounter with a big cat, no doubt. There were three piggies around the size of Gikuyu, Makena, and Wanjiro. And eight tiny piglets. All grazing in a berry patch. They nudged each other affectionately.

I sighed. My sounder was off somewhere grazing just like that, taking comfort in each other's company, living a good piggy life. And here I was, alone, living a boar's life.

It wasn't fair.

A piglet squeaked. Another joined him. Then the whole lot of them squeaked. Three sows ran to the piglets, who were just tall enough to nurse standing up.

The fourth sow stood with the three medium-size

piggies. I got a better look at her now. She was adult, but young. No older than me. Broad and muscular and downright beautiful.

She noticed me. Her little eyes glistened. But she didn't squeal. She didn't alert the older sows.

This beautiful young sow was the only female of her season. Her brothers and male cousins born in the same season must have been driven away— like Mother drove away Kebiro and Mathani and me.

Or maybe she wasn't the only female of her season. Maybe she was the only one who had survived. After all, it was clear this sounder had lost little ones. There were three mother sows, but only three medium-size piggies. And look at those tiny piglets. I counted only eight. Every mother sow had at least three piglets and often four or more. Already this sounder had lost at least one piglet.

This sounder was nowhere near as good at survival as my sounder.

For a moment the ways of the world lay in front of me in dazzling and tragic clarity. If every pig litter grew to old age, the savanna would be overrun with warthogs. In the dry season they'd all suffer cruelly from hunger—there simply wouldn't be enough tubers and roots and rhizomes to feed them all. So the predators had to win now and then. That was the balancing job of nature.

There was no point railing against this conundrum. That was the way it was. That was the way it always had been. That was the way it always would be.

I looked back at the female piggy and hoped upon hope that she would live a long, healthy life. Let her be the exception, the one who made it to a hoary old age.

Her and that crazy baboon. Let them both thrive.

A wet wind rose. The hairless piglets shivered. The sows moved closer together, dragging the nursing babies with them. The adolescent piggies joined the outside of the huddle. They blocked the breeze from the sensitive babies. Their body heat protected those babes.

The young adult sow didn't move, though. She stayed looking at me. The wind ruffled her mane. Her eyes left me confused. And full of energy.

A mother sow followed her gaze. She let out a loud alarm grunt. The other two nursing sows grunted as well. They prepared to charge me.

I trotted away without looking back.

Who needed a sounder, anyway? I was fine by myself. I foraged successfully. Why, this morning I had even eaten a fish. I bet none of the pigs in that sounder had ever tasted a fish. And I had my burrows if I needed to hide.

Oops. I didn't have burrows; I had one burrow.

Sounders never had only one burrow. They had eight, nine, ten. When a predator chased, they ran for the nearest burrow.

I needed more burrows, and now, even though my snout was still sore from yesterday's work.

I searched. Finally, at midday, I found an abandoned burrow. I passed the rest of the afternoon widening the entrance tunnel and dreading the job ahead of widening the inner chamber.

But when I got to the chamber, it was huge. My other aardvark burrow had had a teeny chamber—big enough for only a single aardvark. This one was palatial. It could hold maybe twenty aardvarks. And I realized immediately that I couldn't call this burrow my own. It was perfect for multiple litters. If a sow came across it, she'd kick me out just like that.

I had done all that work for nothing.

I went back up the tunnel. It was late afternoon.

"Wahoo," came the call.

I wasn't surprised. There was that baboon, his rump on a log, his hind legs dangling.

I moved away from the entrance and he scooted past me, down that tunnel. I'd never seen a baboon go into a burrow before. Baboons were great hiders, everyone knew that. But they hid as high as possible. Everyone knew that, too.

In a flash, he came bounding out again, snorting and spitting and brushing the dirt from his head.

I laughed. That's what he got for being so curious. I trotted for home.

The baboon loped past me. He cut off toward the acacia stand where I had first seen him.

I kept trotting, and came across a berry patch. I stopped for a bite. The fruit was juicy and sweet.

A memory came—of a baboon tribe rejoicing in a berry patch. I was little when I saw them. Baboons might eat all kinds of things, but if my memory meant anything, they loved berries most.

I ripped off a berry-laden branch and trotted back toward the acacia stand.

Sure enough, there was that baboon tail, twitching.

I laid the branch of berries under the tail and trotted up the incline to watch.

The baboon leaped to the ground, stood on his hind legs, and looked at me. Then he grabbed the berry branch and swung up into the tree again. "Wahoo," he called, and his voice was wet and sweet with berry juice.

Ha. Two could play at this game.

I trotted home, distinctly happy.

CHAPTER FIFTEEN

Herds and Tribes

IN THE morning a stack of blue water lilies awaited me at the opening of my burrow. I sniffed at them hesitantly. What warthog had ever eaten a water lily?

On the other hand, this was a gift. And the giver might be watching.

I nibbled a petal. Hmm. Like wild onion grass, but tangier. I ate the whole pile. "Thanks," I shouted, just in case.

Then I trotted off in search of a
giraffe herd.

I skidded to a terrified halt.

The monster dog stood in
my path. Blood smeared the fur
down the front of his throat and
chest. He was alone. Like the
time he attacked the ratel.

He blinked, and I saw in that
instant that he recognized me, too.
His eyes narrowed. His nostrils flared.
His chest and leg muscles bunched together
for an attack.

It didn't make sense. He couldn't be hungry;
anyone could see he'd just made a kill. And wild
dogs didn't bury carrion for later. Mother had told
us that.

Still, this dog lowered his head and thrust it forward. He took a step.

Would he kill me just to kill—not to eat? That
was unheard of.

He took another step.

I couldn't possibly outrun him. "Stop!" I
yelped.

His face looked stunned. He lifted his head.

"These tusks can slice through your throat," I said as fiercely as I could. "Why not choose to live one more day, instead?"

He stood there unblinking. I wasn't even sure he had understood. I waited. After a few moments, he disappeared into the brush.

I went weak with relief. But that relief was only temporary. The fact was now beyond doubt: this dog pack was not moving on to new territory. They definitely had a taste for warthog.

I trotted, my heart noisier in my ears than my hoofbeats.

A rustle came from the grasses to my right. I turned quickly. A flash of brown and black disappeared in the brush. The monster dog was keeping up with me from the side.

And he was between me and my burrow.

I trotted faster.

Soon enough I spied a tall spotted neck. Giraffes! Three of them. So few. Usually giraffes clustered in a herd of at least seven or eight. But these three looked healthy and strong. Quiet, mighty giants.

I trotted out to the small herd and stayed alert.

I didn't sense the monster dog's presence any-more, though. He must have left. Hurrah for giraffe hooves; they kept dogs at bay.

Gradually, I calmed down and grazed.

The giraffes ambled at a slow pace, so I had plenty of time to graze and still keep up. I loved watching them eat. They stuck out their long tongues and wrapped them around a cluster of leaves and yanked. My tongue was a clumsy blob in comparison.

"Great tongues," I called up to the giraffe whose head I stood under.

The young cow swayed her slender neck. "Why, thank you, toothy fellow." Her words came melodically and with that regal air only a giraffe could carry off properly.

She made me feel at ease. Still, I scanned the grasses for traces of the monster dog. Nothing. The day went by with a growing sense of ease. No pred-ators showed themselves. Nothing at all happened. It didn't even rain. The sun shined almost as hot as before the rainy season started. The world seemed empty.

In the middle of the day, the giraffes stopped at

the riverbank. They looked around and paced past each other. Their necks made crisscross patterns in the air.

"The leaves are dry today," lamented the old cow. "I'm parched."

"Pity," answered the bull. "I'm afraid drinking is unavoidable."

"I don't see any crocodiles," said the young cow, staring in the water. "Wretched things."

The old cow's neck swayed back and forth. "No crocodiles," she said. But she didn't seem totally convinced.

I examined the water myself. It was thick with lotus blossoms, the same kind Baboony had left for me this morning: blue water lilies. "No crocodiles," I said.

"Does anyone perchance spy a lion?" called the bull.

"No," called back the cows. "Not a one."

"No," I said. "Not a one."

Still, all three kept pacing and eyeing the thickets warily. I didn't understand. Those thickets were so distant that even if a lioness burst from one, the giraffes would have plenty of time to race away.

"For safety's sake," said the bull, "might we go through the strategies?"

"Attention, please," called the younger cow. "Recall, if you will, strategy number one. Run."

"Run," repeated the others.

"Run," I said.

"Attention, please," called the old cow. "Recall, for the benefit of all, strategy number two. Kick."

"Kick," repeated the others.

I'd never seen a warthog kick an enemy. But it seemed only comradely to continue joining in. "Kick," I said.

"A brief review now, my darlings," bellowed the bull. "Run. Kick."

"Run," they repeated. "Kick."

"Run," I repeated with abandon, happy to include myself in his darlings. "Kick."

The bull finally looked satisfied. He splayed his front and back legs in the dirt and lowered his neck toward the river. But his head was still too high to reach the water. A front hoof clumped to one side. The other front hoof clumped to the other side. He spread his front legs that way farther and farther. *Clump clump. Clump clump.* It was a slow, laborious

process, and to me it
looked downright
painful. At last, his
protruding top lip
touched. But his
bottom lip was
still too high.
He spread his
front legs even
farther. The stance
was outrageously
awkward. But his
muzzle was in the water now. He drank. I wanted
to cheer, I was so happy he had made it. But the
others were silent, so I held my tongue.

The cows now performed the same, difficult
routine.

All three of them drank deeply, so splay-legged,
you'd think they could never get up again.

That was it, of course. That was why they
were so nervous. It would take a lot of time to pull
those long legs back into position for running. And
in that time, a lion could latch onto a giraffe neck.
When they drank, the towering animals were as

vulnerable as any other creature.

Which meant that when they drank, the probability of a lion attack was at its highest. And that meant that when they drank, I shouldn't stick around.

I was about to leave when *Plop!* A baby giraffe dropped from the old cow. Wow, she had just given birth.

The calf took a deep, raspy breath and opened his eyes. His legs scrabbled around until he managed to get to a sitting position. He straightened his long neck and looked around with wonder. Though he had fallen a long way, he didn't seem the least bit hurt. Thank heavens his mother's legs were splayed, or he'd have dropped on his head from even higher up.

The adults meanwhile gave no acknowledgment of the marvelous event. They drank and drank.

"Hey," I called. "You've got a son."

The old cow looked around sideways at me. Water dripped from her lips. "A son? That's perfectly lovely." She went back to drinking.

The bull and the young cow didn't even look up.

Oh dear. I couldn't leave now. There was no

one watching the calf. I ran back and forth in a wide arc around the drinking giraffes. "Drink fast. He needs you."

The old cow looked around again. "He shouldn't. Not for quite a while. And if I don't imbibe thoroughly, I won't be able to feed him properly." Her muzzle dipped into the water.

I scanned the thickets. They were so distant that even if several lions hid there, my eyes wouldn't be able to detect their tawny yellow. But at least if a lion did emerge, I could call the alarm immediately.

The giraffes drank.

The baby sat quietly.

I stared at the thickets, only daring to blink when my eyes got so dry they burned.

At long last, the giraffes clumped their legs back together and stood normally. The old cow walked around her son, sniffing hard. Then she licked him tenderly. The bull and the young cow watched with gentle looks on their faces.

Finally the calf got to his feet. He was tall. Double my height, at least. He walked awkwardly but staunchly beside his mother. He was strong.

This was a healthy family.

I trotted away. A feeling of sweet contentment enveloped me. When—oh! There, in a stand of acacias the giraffes had fed from that morning, perched a small tribe of olive baboons, whooping to each other.

Where was Baboony? He needed to meet this tribe. He needed to join them. A lone baboon was a dead baboon.

I searched the area. No Baboony.

I raced back to the acacia stand where Baboony usually stayed. Sure enough, there was his tail, dangling like a beacon. I stood under him and snorted. "Hey, Baboony."

He dropped a newly formed acacia seedpod on my head.

The goofball. "I'm not hungry. I have a surprise."

Baboony lowered his eyelids halfway and looked bored, like he had when he gave me the fish.

"Come with me," I said.

Baboony blew between loose lips, making a blubbery noise. He turned his back on me.

I should have just told him about the other baboons, but I was a little afraid that he might not come then. After all, I didn't really know why he lived alone. "Please come."

"Wahoo," said Baboony. He climbed higher.

"What's up with you? Why don't you talk?"

"Wahoo," said Baboony.

Well, if that was how he wanted it, I'd give it a try. I cleared my throat and made a loud wahoo. Only it came out as "gaaaa."

Baboony looked alarmed. He swung down to a lower branch and peered at me as though I was choking.

"You'll be glad if you come," I said, and I trotted away from the tree.

When I looked back, Baboony was watching me.

I returned to his tree. Then I trotted away again, this time farther.

Baboony was still watching.

I returned to his tree once more. Then I trotted away again, over the incline and out of his line of sight. I stopped and waited.

Baboony appeared at the top of the incline.

Good old Baboony.

I trotted slowly.

Baboony followed.

I stopped a safe distance from the baboon tribe and turned around.

Baboony looked past me at the frolicking tribe. His eyes were as sad and full of longing as any eyes I'd ever seen. Why didn't he rush to them?

Well, there was nothing else I could do. I trotted homeward.

A stick cracked in the nearby brush.

Monster?

I cantered. Then I galloped.

And a sudden resolve came: no more walking or easy trotting for me. I would become the fastest warthog on the savanna.

Monster would never get me.

CHAPTER SIXTEEN

Monster

THE NEXT dawn there were more blue water lilies. Scrumptious.

I ate and started out at a gallop. I quickly tired. But I kept running. Endurance was as important as speed. Wild dogs had both, so I needed both.

By the time I found the giraffes, I was all tuckered out. I staggered stupidly through their legs, circling the dear little calf for a long while before I finally had enough energy to forage.

The giraffes moved lazily. Peacefully. That actually struck me as odd. I'd come to realize that peace on the savanna was a rare thing. Someone was always hungry. Someone was always in danger.

But I wasn't in danger. I could feel peaceful, too, as long as I stayed by the giraffes.

Storm clouds gathered, gray and fat. Rain would soften the earth. That would make tunnel work easier. All right, then, I had a plan: I'd eat till it rained. Then I'd go burrow-hunting.

For now, I breathed deeply of the fine mix of scents. Some plants were still in bloom. Many were already fruiting. The air was lush with their offerings.

And with something else, too. I heard the tribe before I saw them; happy little whoops preceded them across the plain. Olive baboons. This was the tribe I saw yesterday, but I hadn't dared to look them over closely then. Baboon tribes were formidable; warthogs never cozied up to them.

I moved under the young giraffe cow and peered out at the baboon tribe from the safety of this position.

The calf watched me. He moved under his

mother and peered out from between her legs.

"Ah, my heart's delight, my bundle of love," murmured the old cow, "are you frightened? They're just baboons. We are giraffes. We like baboons."

"We like zebras and wildebeests, too," said the young cow. "We're amiable." She peeked down at me with a meaningful look on her face.

The little calf looked at me.

I wasn't about to venture out. I looked away.

The little calf stayed under his mother.

I searched the baboon tribe. I didn't see Baboony anywhere.

The tribe moved in an organized fashion. Adult males marched in front, followed by youngsters, then puffed-up, tough-looking males who were clearly the dominant fellows of the tribe, and then mothers with babies, and finally adolescents about the age of Baboony.

I looked closer. All the adolescents were female. Were the young males driven off, like warthog boars are driven off?

Oh, that's how Baboony wound up alone. He was in exile. And that's why he was sad when I showed him this tribe the day before. Poor Baboony.

The baboon babies were delightful—black with bright pink faces and bright pink rumps. A mother held the teeniest one against her stomach with one hand. Others rode on their mothers' backs, clinging with hands and feet. Older ones tested their independence by jumping off their mothers' backs for a moment, then jumping on again.

The giraffe calf watched as intently as I did. "They're a rowdy crowd," he said softly.

"Not all creatures have the decorum of stately giraffes," said the old cow in an approving tone.

"But baboons are charming in their own way," said the young cow. "Don't you agree?"

"Baboons are fine fellows," said the bull.

And with that, the three adults returned to browsing in the tops of the trees, and the calf nursed.

The baboons settled close by, and reorganized themselves. The dominant males and the mothers with babies stayed in the center. The youngsters and adolescents and less-dominant males surrounded them.

The tiniest baboon baby now hung from his mother's belly as she sifted through the grasses, popping grasshoppers into her mouth. The other really little ones stayed on their mothers' backs and happily smacked their lips at flying insects. The bigger babies rolled around with each other, chasing and poking. Youngsters danced around these babies, stopping between bouts of feeding to join the play. Everyone but the nursing babies seemed to eat anything they found, snatching with their hairless black hands and sometimes even with their feet: grass, leaves, seeds, buds, stalks, nuts, insects, spiders, slugs, lizards. I nodded in agreement; all that was good food.

"Wahoo," came Baboony's call.

I looked up. He was perched in the closest acacia tree. All I could see was his face, sticking out from the leaves, watching the tribe.

The less dominant males jumped to attention. They strutted and chattered. They stopped and, with a glare, sized up Baboony. They showed their teeth. My skin rippled with anxiety.

But all at once the young males gave up that nonsense and went back to feeding.

As soon as they stopped, Baboony leaped down from the tree and came running through the grasses on his hind legs. His arms were outstretched, his elbows crooked, exactly the way he held himself when he ran across the river and caught that mudfish. This time, though, his hands weren't empty: they clutched bouquets of blue water lilies.

The whole tribe stared, dumbfounded. A dominant male barked. The rest of the males squinted and laid their ears flat against their heads.

Baboony spun in a circle and threw flowers

into the air. They showered down on an adolescent female and the mother beside her, who was cradling a teeny baby. For an instant, no one moved. Then youngsters raced up, grabbed the flowers, and skittered away.

A male made a cough-bark at Baboony.

Baboony loped away, in the direction of the river.

"What do you make of that flower-bearing baboon?" asked the young giraffe cow.

"He might be a lunatic," said the bull. "But I don't see any harm in sticking around to see what happens."

"It's already happening," said the old cow.

She was right. The tribe was getting noisy. Downright raucous, in fact. The adolescent female tried to grab back the flowers. They had landed on her head, after all. But the youngsters stuffed them into their mouths as fast as they could. Bigger ones snatched petals from smaller ones, who screeched and tried to snatch them back. One squabble led to another until the whole tribe was panting and clapping their jaws and sticking out their tongues.

That's when Baboony came skipping back

across the plain. A male gave a low broken grunt. Immediately they all looked at Baboony. His hands held even more lilies. My heart fell in dismay. The giraffe bull was right: what a lunatic.

Baboony ran along the edge of the tribe calling, "Wahoo, wahoo." When he got close to that same adolescent female, he tossed flowers into the air again. Blue lilies showered the little female and the same mother as before.

Now everyone grabbed for flowers. But now there were enough to go around. Mothers nibbled on flowers and looked at Baboony. Males chomped on flowers and looked at Baboony. Youngsters ran out toward Baboony, stopped halfway to show him their rumps, then ran back to the safety of the tribe.

Through all this, Baboony kept his eyes on the adolescent female. She ate lilies with her back turned to him. Baboony scratched his rump and chest at the same time. He looked all around. Then he loped away. This time toward the acacia tree. He ripped a gall off the tree and skipped back with it. He laid it on the ground in front of the adolescent female, then retreated a few steps. Ants ran in busy circles all over it. The female picked up the ant gall. She glanced at

Baboony. With a little wheeze, she hunched over the gall and primly ate ants one by one.

Baboony puffed out his chest and strutted proudly back and forth.

A male screamed and bared his fangs. He swaggered toward the adolescent female. The mother that Baboony had tossed flowers on instantly jumped between the male and the young female. They stood face to face. Everyone else watched. The male finally turned and wiggled his backside at her. Then he moved off. That mother watched him till he was way at the other side of the tribe. She turned to the little female and groomed her. The way she did it, I knew she was the little female's mother.

I bet Baboony knew that, too. Oh! Baboony wasn't just trying to join the tribe; he was courting that female. And he was smarter than I thought. If baboon tribes were anything like warthog sounders, daughters stayed with their mothers. So winning over the mother was half the battle.

"Good for you, Baboony," I called out.

The young giraffe cow suddenly stiffened. I moved out from under her fast. The other two adult giraffes stiffened now, as well. Their ears spread. Their tails twitched. The calf looked up at them, alert and nervous.

Baboony turned on his hind legs and looked the direction the giraffes were looking. I looked too.

Something came into sight. And another. And lots. I couldn't make them out yet. But there was no rumble of hooves. There was just silence, telltale silence.

Baboony gave a loud shrill bark.

The wild dog pack ran through the grasses toward the tribe. That same pack.

The giraffes loped away.

Go, little one, I prayed inside my head. Go go.

The adult male baboons formed a line in front of the tribe. They strutted. They bared their sharp canines. They screamed. Baboony joined the end of the line, screaming his head off.

But the dogs kept coming.

The youngsters and females and baby baboons ran after the giraffes, trying to escape through the brush. The adult males bobbed their heads threateningly at the dogs. They stood rigid, arms stiff, with knuckles on the ground. They slapped the earth and showed their teeth.

But the dogs kept coming.

The males now turned and ran, too, shrieking behind the females.

"Wahoo," called Baboony. He loped to the front of the fleeing tribe and led them. "Wahoo, wahoo."

One mother baboon and her baby got separated in the confusion.

The dogs instantly turned as a unit to chase that mother and baby. I knew they would. Poor doomed mother and babe.

All this time I'd been watching as if frozen to the spot. Now I ran the same direction that the baboons ran. After all, that was the direction of the palatial aardvark burrow.

And there it was, just ahead.

I looked over my shoulder to check on that unfortunate mother and baby.

Monster was gaining on them, only moments away from the kill. But for some inexplicable reason, he turned his head right then and glanced my way. Our eyes locked. He veered away from the

baboon mother and baby and came tearing after
me. A few other dogs broke from the pack and followed his lead.

I ran for the burrow.

And before my incredulous eyes, Baboony
zipped down a hole. Then the rest of the baboons
went hurtling down the many other holes into the
palatial aardvark burrow. Mothers and babies and
youngsters. And that adolescent female. And now
the males. Baboony led them all to safety.

I heard Monster's pants behind me.

I spun around and pushed my rump into the
tunnel opening. I huddled just inside with the tips
of my tusks showing.

Monster stopped. The other dogs with him ran
across the top of the burrow whining. A male took
a step toward me. I jerked my tusks at him. He
jumped away.

The dogs retreated, then ran to the grasses—
back to the rest of the pack, who were probably
already ripping apart their prey.

Only Monster remained. He squatted on all
fours and glared at me. Then he sat up and yowled
his rage.

I didn't understand how it had happened. But I was sure of it now: it had become personal. Monster wasn't after just any old warthog meal; he was after me.

CHAPTER SEVENTEEN

My Sounder

THE DOWNPOUR lasted forever. It splashed me in the face. But I stayed at the opening of the burrow. There was no way I was going to shuffle backward down into a chamber jammed full of baboons. And I didn't yet have the courage to leave.

Eventually, though, my muscles cramped from staying in one position. So I slowly emerged from the burrow.

As if that was the cue, baboon heads popped up from two other holes. They jerked side to side, trying to shake off the rain that still fell, then disappeared again. A second later, baboons came crawling from every hole. They raced through the brush for the nearest stand of trees and climbed fast, spitting and snorting dirt. Poor creatures. Baboons always slept high up. It must have been awful for them to be underground like that.

Baboony went with them.

He had succeeded; the tribe had accepted him.

I was happy for him, really.

But I was envious, too.

Male baboons might be cast out of tribes when they matured, just like male warthogs. But male baboons had it better than boars; their job was to find another tribe to join, while we boars had to live out the rest of our lives alone.

I sighed.

One last baboon came out of the burrow, moving lumpily. A dominant male. He looked back at the grasses where we had been attacked. The dog pack had gone. The rain had washed away the traces of their meal.

The male stared, immobile. Then he slumped to his haunches. His head sank into his neck. His eyes were pools of misery.

That must have been his mate and his baby that the pack had eaten.

My heart hurt for him. I hated those dogs. And I hated Monster most of all.

I ran all the way home.

For the next few mornings I raced from my burrow at full speed out to a foraging spot. Ate like a fiend. Then ran home at full speed.

In the afternoons I raced in a wide circle around my burrow entrance, lap after lap after lap, then I dashed inside. Each day I did more laps than the day before, and each day I strayed farther from my burrow than the day before. I got stronger and stronger. Monster would never catch me. Never never.

After three weeks of this routine, I saw a sounder. A big one. Even from a distance, it seemed distinctly familiar. I trotted closer. Then I stopped. A sow ran along one edge of the sounder, spraying urine on rocks. A beautiful, sleek, mature sow.

Behind her ran a strong, young boar, spraying everywhere the sow had sprayed. Mother. And Gikuyu.

I remembered how I had marked territory with Mother not so long ago. Now it was Gikuyu's turn.

It would be a short turn. This time next year, Gikuyu would be off on his own.

My heart broke. For me. For Gikuyu. For all warthog boars everywhere.

I should have left immediately. The sows in that sounder were formidable. If they charged me, it wouldn't be pleasant.

But I had to know.

There was a little hillock nearby that would offer a better viewing point. Hillocks like those, however, were favorite resting spots for lions. I took a deep breath.

I had to know. I absolutely had to.

I climbed the hillock. Lucky me, no one was there. I looked out over the sounder. And there was a trim, pretty piggy—Makena, my dear sister. And now I recognized my aunts. And cousins. And there were so many new piglets scattered throughout the bigger piggies. Which were Mother's?

An aunt spotted me and gave off an alarm grunt.

The whole sounder went nuts. Sows raced off with strings of piglets and piggies behind them. I watched Mother run, followed by four piglets, then Gikuyu and Makena and Wanjiro. Poor Wanjiro— very last of all, just like I used to be.

At that moment Wanjiro looked back. My littlest sister, the one who said I was the most cautious, who relied on my opinion. She looked right at me. And she stopped and let out an explosive grunt of joy.

Mother turned then. So did Makena and Gikuyu and the four piglets. They all stopped and stared at me.

"You look good," I called. "The whole family looks good."

"So do you, Mogo," called Mother. "Different, but good." She opened her mouth again. Then she closed it. She didn't ask about Kebiro or Mathani. Of course not; she could guess. "Good-bye, Mogo," called Mother.

"Good-bye," called Gikuyu and Makena and Wanjiro.

"Good-bye," called the tiny piglets.

"Good-bye," I said.

"Live well," called Mother.

They turned and disappeared.

They were safe: Mother and her new piglets and the year-old piggies. I had found out what I wanted to know.

And they still loved me. Even if I couldn't live with them.

I wandered away into the grasses again, eating slowly, savoring the memory of my fine, healthy family.

When, oh, there was a second sounder. A little one this time. It was the same sounder I'd seen three weeks ago. The one with the four adult females, the three year-old piggies, and the eight tiny piglets. Except there weren't that many anymore. There were three adult females, three year-old piggies, and only five piglets. What?

I had to be mistaken; this had to be a different sounder. But, no, there was the scar across the rump of one of the sows. And, oh, yes, there was that beautiful young sow. Stunning, actually.

A squeal burst from me.

The whole sounder looked up in alarm.

The young female squealed back.

One of the mother sows moved in front of her and scowled at me. She let out a threatening grunt.

The young female moved to the side, so that we held each other in full view again. She didn't scowl. She didn't grunt.

"Wahoo."

Way over across the grasses, tails hung from an

acacia tree. Baboony was with his tribe. But he was still calling to me. We were still friends.

My friend was now happy. I wanted to be happy, too.

I didn't realize till now how good life used to be when I wandered with the giraffes. There was pleasure in listening to them. Even pleasure in worrying about that little calf. Company offered so much pleasure. Since that last dog pack attack, life had become nothing but the determination to stay out of Monster's jaws.

This was a conundrum I could not accept. I would not. What was the point if life was no fun at all?

Mother said to live well. All right, I would. I definitely would.

I raced to the river. Near the middle, blue water lilies floated in profusion. I tore some up, then raced back to the sounder. I left them on the ground nearby and trotted away to watch from a safe distance.

The sounder put their heads together. Then the beautiful female trotted over to the water lilies. She looked up at me.

"Lilies," I called encouragingly.

She took a bite and chewed thoughtfully. Then she ate more.

The other pigs joined her. They all ate blue petals.

It was a perfect moment.

I took a few slow steps toward the sounder and paused. They chewed contentedly.

Maybe they would really accept me. My heart thumped hard.

I took a few more steps.

And, no, not again! Monster came trotting through the grasses, like everything bad and wrong merging in one form. He was alone. It was late morning so the pack had surely already hunted, already fed. But here he was. I knew he'd been following me. He was always following me.

The sounder went nuts. They scattered. The fools. No wonder they kept getting picked off by predators.

"There's a burrow over to the right," I shouted. "Go for it."

The young female ran where I said. But the rest of them ran randomly.

"All of you, go for it," I shouted. "All of you!"

The three piggies followed the female. And one sow. And three piglets.

But the other sow and her two piglets ran the wrong way.

Monster ran toward them.

No! Last time the dog pack got that mother and baby baboon because I was too slow and stupid to save them. But I could run faster now. I was the fastest piggy in the history of the savanna, I was sure of it. I could do this. All I needed was courage.

I dashed between Monster and the sow with her piglets.

"Go!" I shouted at her. "Go after the others! Fast!"

Monster hesitated for an instant, then he pulled his eyes from the piglets and chased me, instead.

The sow and piglets headed for the burrow, and they were slow. That meant I couldn't run for the burrow, because I'd soon pass them and then Monster would get them. I had no choice but to outrun him in the other direction.

I ran and dodged and ran and dodged and ran

and dodged. I was fast and strong. But Monster was still faster and stronger. He gained on me by the second.

I ran under an acacia tree.

Plop! A huge mass of gray dropped down on Monster. It was Baboony! He seized Monster around the neck, and bit him in the throat. They rolled. Blood spurted. Teeth flashed. A scream shook the leaves.

A giant baboon dropped to the ground beside them and bit Monster's head clear off.

I saw it all, but I kept running, racing through the acacia trees, glancing back anxiously, expecting Monster's teeth to sink into my flank. I ran and ran, in crazy, senseless loops. I ran till I couldn't anymore.

Then I saw for real. And I knew. Monster was now a baboon meal. The males ripped him apart. Baboony among them.

Monster was dead.

Just like that. In an instant all that horrible stuff had ended.

Baboony had saved me. Baboony and that huge male baboon.

And I had saved the sow and her two piglets.

I stood in one spot for a long time. The ropes of worry that had held me tight all these weeks since Mother had cast my litter out of the sounder gradually loosened and fell away. I wasn't the same piggy I had been back then. Mother was right; I was different. Faster and stronger. But it was more than that. Much more.

I turned and trotted slowly toward the palatial burrow. The sounder safely nestled down there. I wouldn't be welcome inside, I knew that. So I stopped nearby.

Piglet squeals came from the burrow. Piggy grunts. Wonderful sounds of life.

Monster was dead.

Maybe he had a mate who would cry for him. And pups who would search for him in a daze. But they were part of a pack; they wouldn't starve, they wouldn't be left unprotected.

Without me, though, this sounder would have been unprotected.

Monster was gone, but there would be other threats. Other hungry predators.

I looked around carefully, stamped my hooves, and grazed. The pigs in that burrow were alive.

I wanted them to stay that way.

"Grunt." The young sow poked her head out of a burrow hole. "You're here."

"I'm here."

"Are you keeping guard?"

"Of course," I said. And it was true. That was exactly what I was doing.

"Thank you."

"You're welcome."

She disappeared inside.

Then she reappeared. "The water lilies were unusual."

She disappeared again.

Then she reappeared again. "They were good. That's what I meant to say."

"I'm glad you liked them."

She disappeared once more.

I waited, hoping she'd come back.

When she didn't, I wandered a little, never too far, grateful for the knowledge that my sounder was safe.

My sounder.

What a surprising thought. But that was what they were. I had an old sounder, the one I'd grown up with, and a new sounder, this one. But this was the one I'd stay with.

I couldn't nuzzle up to them in a burrow. I couldn't even graze close to them. But I could watch over them. With my help, these piggies and piglets had a chance at growing up.

This might not be the warthog way, but who knew? Maybe it was. Maybe there were warthog boars looking out for sounders all over this savanna. All over Africa. All over the world. Without the sows being any the wiser.

Maybe there was a boar looking out for Mother and her piggies and new piglets, and for my entire old sounder. Oh, I hoped so.

But even if no other boar had ever done this,

even if no other boar ever would again, I was going to. This was my life. I would work as hard to save my sounder as to save myself.

I would bring them blue water lilies every rainy season.

I knew it wouldn't work for me like it had worked for Baboony. Warthogs weren't baboons. I would never be accepted into their midst. But giving gifts was fun.

Ah, there was more to life than survival. There was living well.

I grazed, joyful at the whole miraculous adventure.